GRAVE ROBBERS

Doc Beck Westerns Book 3

SARAH ELISABETH SAWYER

GRAVE ROBBERS
Grave Robbers © 2021 by Sarah Elisabeth Sawyer
All rights reserved.

RockHaven Publishing
P.O. Box 1103
Canton, Texas 75103

Editor: Lynda Kay Sawyer
Cover Design: Mollie E. Reeder
Author Photo by R. A. Whiteside. Courtesy of the National Museum of the American Indian, Smithsonian Institution

ISBN: 978-1-956043-00-6

The alcove in the saloon wasn't the most inconspicuous place for a life-and-death meeting on a Sunday night, but it would do.

Alone in the alcove, for now, Dirk Ferguson leaned back in his chair, tipping onto its back legs. He raised his feet and stabbed his spur on the green cloth-covered table, crossing one foot over the other. A foaming mug in hand, he watched the crowded bar through the beaded curtain that separated the alcove from the rest of the saloon.

This became Dirk's favorite hang-out and meeting place after he was old enough to beat up his pa and leave their ramshackle claim. He drifted to Hagan, a spit of a town that saw its peak long ago with the California gold rush.

Dirk's boss, Harold Monahan, was good to him, giving him a place to live in a shed out back of his home. The best part was the easy jobs Monahan gave him here and there. They always paid well.

Harold Monahan dealt from the bottom of the deck more often than not in this town. But, as long as Dirk covered for him, no one dared point it out. Dirk wasn't intimidating in size; it was his fast and accurate draw that made everyone give him a wide berth.

No one besides Dirk knew all of Monahan's dirty little secrets. And here was the dirtiest one—a young man named Willy, walking through the beaded curtain of the alcove. He brought a whiff of cigarette smoke with him from the men at the bar.

At least Willy had enough wits about him to follow Dirk's instructions to meet him there so Dirk could calm him down.

Willy's pale skin was slick as a silk handkerchief, sweat glistening on his forehead. He sat across from Dirk, his hands clenched together in a fist.

"You got to do something." Willy's words came out like a gasp. "Thad Biggins is going to fetch a doctor to do an autopsy. What if they find out..."

The coward looked like he was going to vomit. But Dirk's chance for cashing in one last time with Monahan and getting out of that town was coming.

A big part of Dirk's job was keeping Willy's mouth shut. Ruby Palmer had only been dead twenty-four hours, and this young man—bound for an Ivy League school—hadn't recovered from the shock.

Dirk rolled his feet off the table and they landed with a thump next to Willy, who jerked like the spurs had cut him. Dirk leaned forward, handing his mug to Willy, who took it with shaking hands. Those hands were going to put a noose around Willy's neck unless Dirk played their cards just right.

"I told you I'd take care of everything, didn't I?" Dirk asked, quiet and calm. "That dirty bandit killed Ruby and all the town knows it. Don't they?"

Willy gulped from the mug. "But the trial... it shouldn't be happening so fast, should it?"

Dirk chuckled. "Owen Palmer is the one pushing for that, and I reckon we know why. He'd have done it to Ruby if you hadn't. He'll be on our side if that doctor does find anything out."

A drop of sweat trickled down Willy's temple. Dirk loosened his bandanna, popped it open, and handed it to him.

"All you got to do is stay calm," Dirk said. "They'll convict that bandit tomorrow and hang him before sundown. Folks in this stupid town will be flying high with the fact that they served out good old-fashioned, western justice. It'll be over and done with. Ruby Palmer will be remembered as a fine, upstanding young lady, even though everyone knows the truth. It'll give them a good story to tell of how the whole town came to her defense. No one will dare give any more thought to it. You trust me."

"But Deputy Biggins and that doctor...what do we do about them?"

Dirk rested his elbows on his knees and looked directly at Willy, who refused to meet his eyes. "You swing just as high for killing one as you do three."

Willy's head came up, his eyes bulging. Dirk shouldn't have voiced what Harold Monahan didn't say aloud, either. Time to calm Willy down again.

Dirk Ferguson leaned his chair back casually and propped his boots on the table. He stabbed the table with his spur and rolled it forward, cutting the green cloth. The only thing he liked about this town—except Monahan's pay—was that the saloon didn't close on Sundays.

"If Judge George Slater hadn't stepped in, saying things needed to be done proper for the record, Sheriff Eden would've let the town lynch that bandit yesterday," Dirk said. Then he grinned at the real killer. "But we're holding a pat hand. You got nothing to worry about. You're even on the jury."

CHAPTER 1

The train lulled Doctor Rebekah LaRoche into a mid-morning catnap. The more years that passed in her life, the easier she could fall asleep almost anywhere. That was a good thing for a doctor who often found herself up at all hours of the day and night.

Rebekah could use the rest before entering the town of Hagan. It held one of Sancho Guerra's bandits, who escaped the mission in Zapata.

Was the identification a mistake, and the accused murderer of the young woman Ruby Palmer someone else entirely? Or was Rebekah about to encounter Pinto Diaz, Edgardo Guerra, or Sancho Guerra himself?

She truly hoped it wasn't Edgardo. He was hardly more than a boy, and there was a decency about him that could lead him to a better life. If he wasn't hanged first.

Rebekah blinked and stretched her arms in front of her. Deputy Thad Biggins, on the passenger seat across from her, remained quiet, seeming in a world of his own as he gazed out the train window. He was a fine-looking young man, showing his mixed heritage in his skin tinted brown and his thin lips.

After coming to Zapata to ask Rebekah to do an autopsy for a murder case in his town, he said little about the case other than the victim's name and how her body was in the town ice house for keeping until burial.

Just Jimmy, still faithfully at her side, had drifted off to sleep, which was better than him fidgeting. He was anxious to get to Wyoming, but truth be told, the delay was welcome for Rebekah. She wasn't ready to go back there yet.

Hagan was two stops down from Zapata, taking them south which went along with Sancho Guerra's escape path. Rebekah tried not to think of how, if Sancho wasn't the accused in jail, that he might still be close around.

The train pulled into the Hagan depot and Jimmy awoke with the jerk of the car. The three disembarked onto the dusty platform with the red New Mexican mesas stretched across the desert around them. A town like this would be hard-pressed to exist without a railroad bringing lumber for the false-fronted buildings. The world was changing fast, making room for new possibilities as a new century loomed. Rebekah was content in the old one for now.

Jimmy carried their carpetbags with her medical bag tucked under one arm at his insistence. She allowed him to carry the full weight because she knew he wanted to feel useful. And he was a strong young man, even as wiry as he was. But he knew nothing about medical procedures, so he couldn't assist her in things like an autopsy. She'd find other tasks to keep him busy while they were in Hagan.

Deputy Biggins led them to the end of the platform but halted. Rebekah caught a look of dejection cross his face, as though he just incurred a parent's displeasure.

She followed his gaze to see a young man striding toward them, his sheriff's badge catching a glint of sunshine. The sheriff, rugged and angry looking, took the low platform steps in one bound to come nose to nose with his deputy.

"Biggins, I didn't give you leave to run off with all we got going on here."

Biggins pulled his mouth into a tight line. "Was someone else murdered?"

The sheriff's eyes flashed with dark amusement. "You got a point there. That girl was murdered on your night watch."

Deputy Biggins blanched, but he held tight to his composure. He politely turned to indicate Rebekah and Jimmy. "Sheriff Eden, this is Doc Beck and her assistant Jimmy. She has agreed to do the autopsy."

The sheriff, easily a decade younger than Rebekah, gave her a dismissive look.

"If it makes you feel better, Biggins," he said. "Get her the body from the icehouse. I got to go back to the saloon. Trial's starting in ten minutes."

Rebekah raised her eyebrows. "The trial is commencing? What about a coroner's inquest?"

Sheriff Eden looked put out that she'd asked not only one, but two questions of him. He narrowed his eyes. "Don't need one. Don't need you. But if you want to testify, you have your results ready by 2 p.m. We're hanging that bandit before sundown once Judge Slater is convinced everything's been done for the records."

Jimmy bristled, looking ready to jump to Rebekah's defense at the sheriff's harsh tone. But Sheriff Eden turned on his heel and strode down the steps and up the dusty street of his town toward the saloon situated in the middle of it. That must be the courtroom for the sham trial.

But it was already past noon. The sheriff's demand was ridiculous.

Rebekah tugged her medical bag out from under Jimmy's arm. She needed to focus on the autopsy, not the surrounding drama, and certainly not on the supposed bandit at the trial now. A tingle went up her spine at the thought that it could be Sancho Guerra.

"Deputy Biggins, it sounds as if we better get started," she said. "I see the sign for the doctor's office down the street. If you'll let us in there and have the body brought, I'll begin. But please know I can't do a thorough examination in such a short amount of time. Would you inform the sheriff of that?"

Deputy Biggins nodded. "Yes ma'am, and you may let yourself in the office. There is a room over the office that you can stay in while you're in town." As he spoke, he dug deep in his trouser pocket, pulled out a set of keys, and handed them to Rebekah. "I'll bring...the body." He started to turn, then halted, his shoulders sagging. He looked back at her. "*Gracias*. Thank you for coming, *Señorita* Beck."

There was a softness in his brown eyes that told Rebekah he had a reason for caring more about this case than the sheriff apparently did.

While Jimmy went to get his horse off the train and into the stables—still carrying both carpetbags— Rebekah walked alone to the doctor's office. A mass of horses and wagons covered the front of the saloon she passed, filling the hitching rail and the alleys on both sides of the building.

But everything was eerily still and silent in the town. Rebekah found herself checking upper story windows, especially of the two-story hotel caddy corner from the doctor's office. What was she looking for? It felt like the town itself was hiding something behind its false fronts and adobe walls.

Then a hammering sound rang out. Something was being built.

Inside the doctor's office, Rebekah took a deep breath and went to the medicine cabinet. Deputy Biggins seemed to have a key to every building in town on his ring, and one of them unlocked the medical cabinet. The town doctor did keep things in neat order, everything Rebekah needed for her work. She would make sure it was all back in place before she left.

At the same time she finished setting up for the autopsy, Jimmy came in, then halted when he saw her ready for work.

He gulped. "Horse is stowed away, Miss Rebekah. What do you need me to do now?"

"It looks as though we'll stay here overnight, so if you'll please take my bag upstairs, you can get yourself a room in the hotel before we need to be at the trial."

"Oh no, Doc," Jimmy waved his hand in the air, color coming back to his face when she didn't ask him to help with the autopsy, at least not yet. "I'll just sleep with my horse at the stable. No use going to all the trouble and expense of a hotel room for me."

Rebekah smiled and said in a teasing tone, "You'll do as I say, young man. You've been a great help to me the past few weeks and I won't have you sleeping in a barn again with the manure. Consider it part of your pay."

Jimmy opened his mouth as though to object, but a thump outside had him turning to open the door. He jumped back and Deputy Biggins entered, carrying the front end of a stretcher. An older man, also sporting a deputy badge, carried the foot end. On the stretcher was a blanket-wrapped body.

Rebekah directed the men to put the stretcher on the exam table. They carefully set it in place and Deputy Biggins took a step back, his tan face as pale as it could be. Rebekah gave him a nod.

"Thank you, Deputy Biggins," she said as she fetched a large gray apron from a hook by the medicine cabinet. "I'll come to the courtroom—the saloon—after my preliminary examination."

The deputy let the older man leave before him. Thad Biggins looked back at the body one last time, then left, quietly closing the door behind him.

Jimmy stood there, motionless, looking green around the gills. Rebekah patted his arm.

"You can wait outside, Jimmy. I'll call if I need you."

Relief splashed Jimmy's face that held so much innocence. He'd seen things in his young years, but the work ahead was beyond what he could, or should, comprehend at his age.

When the office door closed, Rebekah pulled the curtain around the exam table in case anyone came in unexpectedly. She bowed her head, wanting to say a brief prayer, but nothing came to her.

Still, this was sacred work and she would conduct it with respect and care in her heart. She would not rush the process for anyone.

❧

REBEKAH WAS JOLTED by soft tapping on the office door. She glanced at the clock in the corner of the exam area. 2 p.m.

As the door creaked, she covered the body and began washing her hands.

Jimmy called quietly from beyond the blue curtain, "Miss Rebekah? Deputy Biggins is here. Says they want you over at the courthouse now."

"Be there in a moment, Jimmy." Rebekah paused by the exam table, drying her hands and composing herself.

Questions lurked in the recesses of her mind. The main question wasn't in determining the cause of death. The girl was strangled. Rebekah had paused a moment when she discovered that, recalling what it was like to have Sancho's hands clenched around her throat. This was how she would have died.

But there was more to Ruby Palmer's death than the obvious. Rebekah needed more time to put her finger on it.

It didn't look like she was going to get it. A man's life was at stake, though there wasn't anything useful in her testimony. If it were one of the bandits, he would surely hang for something else anyway. All of Sancho's men were killers, except Edgardo.

Would she see him in the courtroom?

Rebekah removed the large gray apron and rolled down the sleeves of her navy-blue dress as she exited through the curtain.

The curtain securely in place, she checked her reflection in the mirror outside the exam area. Her hair was still neat although a few strands had gotten out of place from the train ride and her work. She tucked the dark brown pieces into her bun and tightened the pins.

This was the first time Rebekah was the lead doctor on an autopsy for a criminal case, and she should look professional—even when giving her testimony in a saloon.

Rebekah stepped into the fresh air outside, taking note of the older deputy, who helped carry the body, standing by Deputy Biggins.

She asked the older man, "Will you be staying here to make sure no one disturbs the body until I return, Deputy...?"

He nodded. "Deputy Wallace, ma'am."

Wallace didn't look quite physically capable of wearing the deputy badge, and his voice even cracked. But he did have a seasoned look, though not one that instilled complete confidence.

It was important to protect the vulnerable body, so Rebekah asked Jimmy, "Would you stay here as well and come for me if anyone has a medical need? I can treat patients that come in the doctor's absence while we're here."

"You can count on me, Doc Beck," Jimmy said, taking up his post in the doorway, arms crossed and six-gun in easy drawing position. She wondered how well he could shoot, though there was no reason for that to be tested in this town—unless Sancho Guerra showed up. She shivered. Jimmy did need to be on guard.

Deputy Biggins led Rebekah down the street to the saloon. The urgent hammering sounded again.

Rebekah asked him, "Town expansion?"

He glanced at her then away. "Gallows."

They went in single file through the haphazard mess of horses and wagons, up the boardwalk, and to the saloon doors. The doors were pressed open by the crowd that spilled out onto the boardwalk, doing their best to get a look inside.

Deputy Biggins made a path through the people, Rebekah

close behind him. She caught backhanded whispers as she passed, words about a woman doctor testifying.

The saloon was jam-packed, the bar closed with men using it as a bench for a good seat to see above the gathering. The customary tables were replaced with rows of chairs filled with spectators. Brass spittoons, lingering smoke smell in the air, and alcohol stains on the floor reminded her how fake all this was.

To the right was what looked like the jury box, partially tucked into an alcove. The beaded curtain was tied back, giving her full view of the twelve men sitting in judgment, their faces in fixed expressions. They already found this man guilty but were going along with the proceedings, "for the record" as Sheriff Eden said.

Deputy Biggins led her toward the corner of the room where a hastily built wood platform served as the judge's bench with a small table and chair placed on it. Judge Slater sat slouched, his face shadowed with two day's growth of salt and pepper hair for his beard. A shock of white hair on his head was as untamed as he was—apparently a leftover judge from the wild west.

Not more than ten feet before the bench was another table where Sheriff Eden sat with a shackled man.

The prisoner was huge, well capable of inflicting the damage she'd seen on the young woman's body. This was not Edgardo. Nor Sancho. That much she knew.

But still, when she came around to the side of the table, his profile made her lose her breath.

It was Pinto Diaz, the bandit who had nearly broken Jimmy in half.

CHAPTER 2

The judge, his shock of white hair waving with every word, barked, "Thad, this the doctor you fetched for the autopsy?"

Deputy Thad Biggins stayed at Rebekah's side. "Yes, your honor."

"Well, I got nothing against a woman doctoring folks," Judge Slater said. "My ma doctored me and my cussed brothers, and we all lived."

Light laughter went through the courtroom, alleviating some of the tension. But not the fear inside Rebekah.

She couldn't take her eyes off Pinto Diaz. Sheriff Eden shifted in his chair to scowl at her, and Pinto, on his other side, raised his head. His eyes darted toward her, then he looked down.

Suddenly, his head jerked up and he glared at her, recognizing her without the nun's habit.

He growled in Spanish, "You cursed daughter of a..."

Pinto lunged at her, massive hands shackled but coming up as though to wrap around her throat despite his missing left thumb.

But his legs were shackled, too, causing him to sprawl over the sheriff who leaped to his feet and whipped out his pistol. He brought it down over the bandit's head, flattening him on the floor.

The courtroom erupted and a man shouted, "Hang him! Hang him now!"

Rebekah froze, staring at Pinto's massive frame on the floor as the bandit groaned, blood trickling from the new cut on his head.

She was right—the murderer of Ruby Palmer was not one of Sancho Guerra's gang. It was someone else entirely.

She realized Deputy Biggins had a protective hold of her arm, tugging her back as he stood half in front of her. He glanced down at her, questioning.

Rebekah swallowed and said quietly, "Yes, he is one of the bandits who rode with Sancho Guerra. But this man is not the one who killed Ruby Palmer."

The sheriff straightened, standing about eye level with her. He heard what she said.

"What do you mean?" he hissed. "How could you possibly know that?"

Judge Slater banged on his gavel, then shook it at the sheriff.

"Get these people under control, Barney Eden, or I'll clear them all out of here."

Sheriff Eden turned toward the crowd and cut his arms in the air several times.

"Shut up and sit down, all of you!" he shouted. "We're almost through with this trial and you'll see the murderer hang soon enough."

He said the last part while looking at Rebekah, his eyes holding a warning look. He had this case tied up with a bow and she was not to interfere.

But she must. Pinto Diaz was guilty as sin, but not of Ruby Palmer's death. She couldn't let that stand in a court of law, if that was what the town wanted to call this.

There was one person in the room to appeal to who could give her a chance to tell the truth. She lifted the hem of her navy-blue skirt as she maneuvered around the defense table and Pinto's crumpled body.

She halted before Judge Slater's bench and said, "Your honor, after my initial examination of the body, I have strong reason to believe Pinto Diaz did not kill Ruby Palmer."

The saloon erupted again. Rebekah's testimony would prove Pinto's innocence, but it was doubtful anyone would believe her, and they would lynch him anyway. He deserved it—yet she knew what it was to be accused of something she didn't do and found guilty.

But there was an even stronger reason for what she must do.

Once Sheriff Eden shouted everyone down again, Rebekah continued. "Your honor, I request the trial be postponed long enough for me to complete my examination."

Like a wave rolling in from the ocean, a force shifted the air beside Rebekah. A big man was there on her other side from Deputy Biggins, a mountain equal to Pinto. Despite the tailored, three-piece suit he wore, there was as mean a look as Pinto's in the man's blue eyes. His face was a sheen of sweat—red and angry like a hornet.

He spoke to Rebekah, yet loud enough for all to hear. "I don't know who you think you are, lady, but I will tell you who I am— Owen Palmer, president of the bank that Sancho Guerra's men ravaged on their way to Zapata. They killed my clerk and butchered him. Furthermore, I am Ruby Palmer's stepfather and I will see justice served before this day is over so we can lay her to rest in peace. I don't see you playing a part in that today."

Deputy Biggins shifted from blocking Rebekah from Pinto to putting himself between her and Owen Palmer. Based on his stance and look in his eyes, Thad Biggins had little tolerance for this man. But he kept his tone civil.

"Mr. Palmer, I brought the doctor here to see justice served for Miss Ruby," he said. He paused, then added, "We need to make sure we hang the right man."

Palmer's eyes flashed and he looked like he might strike the deputy. But he glanced around at all the witnesses to the exchange and held himself in check.

Rebekah had seen that kind of power under control, of thinking more of what people thought of what you were doing than what you were actually doing. It never turned out good behind closed doors.

Palmer took a step back and returned to his seat in the center of the room, his boots scraping loud in the silence.

Judge Slater rapped his gavel once then shook it at Rebekah, his shock of hair bobbing. "The little lady has a point. I will hold the trial until the autopsy is complete. For the records."

Protest sounded again and Sheriff Eden said, "Biggins, clear these people out."

Deputy Biggins glanced at Rebekah, an apology in his eyes, but she motioned for him to go on about his duty. She didn't want to wait for the crowd to disperse before making her exit, though. The sheriff and two other men were hefting Pinto onto his feet and she didn't want the bandit to set eyes on her again.

There was a side door to her left and she bumped past a few men to reach it. One man she bumped into sidestepped into her path.

She halted and met his eyes. He was young, but already hard lines creased his forehead with the look of a gunslinger that always found himself still standing after a shootout. What disturbed her most, though, was the way he smiled at her, like he knew every secret in this town and about her.

"Ma'am," he drawled, slow and easy, and Rebekah realized it was the same voice that had shouted for Pinto Diaz to be hanged. "I reckon you know what you got to do. We're hanging that bandit and we sure don't want no one else getting hurt, do we? 'Sides, Ruby was hardly worth this much fuss."

He tipped his hat and strode toward the middle of the saloon. Rebekah turned to follow his path and saw him aim for the juror box as the men in it followed the spectators. The haphazard, angry jurors took turns glaring at her as they left.

But one young man with a pasty white face caught her attention. He was the only one who didn't look at her. Nor did he look displeased about being dismissed.

CHAPTER 3

Near sunset, when the town thought Pinto Diaz would hang on the new gallows, Rebekah sat beside the exam table, the body covered again. Or bodies, to be precise.

Rebekah closed her eyes, the sacredness of human life filling her thoughts and being. These two lives in her presence were taken too soon.

Her father raised her to respect the dead, to look on a body as the evidence of the Creator's most valued creation. She had struggled to balance that need for respect in medical school. But her father, through dictation, wrote letters to her about his pride in the good work that she was doing, and how God understood she did what she must do.

In her class when the students were observing an autopsy being performed for the first time, one of the male students passed out. But Rebekah found herself fascinated with the human body and how marvelous it was. Then she trained under one of the leading doctors who performed autopsies in criminal cases. He went more in-depth than the average physician to discover everything possibly related to the death. His autopsies took longer, same as Rebekah's would, but it was important work.

That the human body was created by a Superior Being was something she must confess in her work that day in Hagan, New Mexico Territory. Even the word *autopsy* meant more to her in the moment. Derived from the Greek *autopsia*, it meant "the act of seeing for oneself."

She only wished that Superior Being took an interest in the pain and longing of her own heart.

Fumes from the alcohol she used to clean her instruments, along with steadily decaying bodies, filled the room. Rebekah went to the doctor's office door and stepped outside, taking a cleansing breath of fresh air.

Tears smarted her eyes. She wasn't finished with the autopsy, but she did need a break. What she had discovered so far shocked and saddened her.

Jimmy was leaned back in a chair to the left side of the door and came to his feet when she appeared.

His eyes widened. "Miss Rebekah, you alright?"

She closed her eyes, realizing he'd never seen her cry. He may even think she never did. How wrong he would be.

"No, Jimmy, I'm not." She opened her eyes, feeling them clear, and smiled at him. "But I will be."

His eyebrows scrunched together, worried. He reached into the inner pocket of his short yellow jacket and pulled out a tiny book. "Maybe you'd like to read this a spell?"

Rebekah looked at the brown leather book, realizing it was a New Testament. Her fingers tingled, wanting to take it. But she said, "You read it for us both, Jimmy."

He grinned and fanned the pages, giving off the scent of a worn, beloved book. "Sure wish I could, ma'am. Never did learn to read."

His confession jolted Rebekah, reminding her of why she had

brought Jimmy along from Texas. He did need someone to finish raising him.

"Were you never in school?" she asked.

Jimmy grinned, that one he used when he was about to take off on a wild yarn. "Yes ma'am, them teachers at the fancy boarding school I went to in Pennsylvania thought I was some kind of scholar. Hardworking, they called me. Just never took to reading. I reckon the good Lord figured I didn't need it."

Rebekah tapped the book. "Be that as it may, I can teach you to read from that book if you want."

Jimmy stood still, mouth open. It was his turn for his eyes to redden with tears. "Would you, Miss Rebekah? Really?"

"Really, Just Jimmy." She breathed deep. "I'm going to take a short walk now. Would you stand guard here?"

"You bet."

Rebekah started to leave, then halted. That sense of foreboding was bothering her again as she glanced up and down the streets of Hagan.

"Jimmy, with Pinto Diaz here, know that Sancho Guerra may be around," she said. "There is a good chance he will attempt to break Diaz out of jail. Please watch out for yourself."

He nodded—his eyes solemn. "I will, while I'm watching out for you."

Rebekah walked down the street that had quieted since the crowd dispersed from the trial. The few people she did encounter seemed to recognize her and gave her scathing looks. One mother drew her child close as though Rebekah was an accomplice in Ruby Palmer's murder.

This town regarded her as its newest enemy.

Rebekah kept going until she reached the building marked *Jail*. Deputy Biggins was seated outside, leaned back in a chair, hat over his eyes, snoozing. She recalled how the sheriff said Deputy Biggins had night watch duty. He would likely go to work patrolling the streets soon.

Rebekah hated to interrupt his sleep, but he brought her into this situation and seemed to be the only one with a level head in this town.

She stepped onto the wooden porch of the jail, and he twitched. He pushed his hat up with one hand, his other hand dropping to his six-gun.

When he saw her, he quickly got to his feet and removed his hat. "Doc Beck. You have finished? Would you like to speak with the sheriff?"

"No, Deputy Biggins, I actually came to see you." Rebekah indicated the empty chair next to his and he made room for her.

After they sat, she asked, "How well did you know Ruby Palmer?"

His face went crimson and his eyes darted up the street as though afraid someone would hear his thoughts.

"As well as anyone in town, Señorita. Miss Palmer was what you might call a loner."

Rebekah noticed how he used Spanish words, and even his accent changed, when speaking with her. He probably thought she was part Mexican like him.

"Who was her closest friend?" she asked.

Deputy Biggins swallowed, turning his hat round in his hands. "Frances Jackson, I think. That's the only girl I remember Ruby being friendly with. There were more young men she was friendly with. "

The last part seemed to slip out before Deputy Biggins could catch himself. His face turned a deeper shade of red.

Rebekah pressed on. "About Frances Jackson who was Ruby's friend. Was she at the trial today?"

"No, señorita. She married a man with a farm about ten miles from here. I do not think she has even heard about Ruby yet—Miss Palmer, that is."

Rebekah studied the young deputy's face. He was easy to read, and she knew he wasn't telling her everything.

There were more questions she had for him, but that was enough for now. She was no detective, but her gut told her Frances Jackson had answers, too.

"Thank you, Deputy Biggins. Would you please have someone move the stretcher back to the icehouse? I'll resume my examination in the morning."

Biggins nodded, not meeting her eyes. "I'll see that it is taken care of."

IN THE RESTAURANT at the hotel, Jimmy reacted stronger than Rebekah expected when she told him she was going to see Frances. He even stopped eating.

"Miss Rebekah, I don't see why you gotta get so involved," he said, his tone between a growl and a plea. "Ain't you supposed to just tell the judge how the girl died and leave all the sheriff work to the sheriff?"

Rebekah took a bite of her chicken and dumplings, chewing slowly. She didn't answer Jimmy. She wanted him to think through the situation for himself.

He squirmed in his seat and finally said, "I'm sorry, Doc. I just...That bandit pert-near killed me. I don't see why you're so sure he didn't kill the girl. I heard folks in town talking about how Pinto was found in an alley near her, passed out drunk and holding her scarf."

Jimmy stabbed his mashed potatoes with his fork then shoveled in a mouthful. One thing about Jimmy, no distress was going to keep him from eating for very long.

He stopped chewing and swallowed. "Is that how he did it? Choked her with her own scarf?"

Rebekah shook her head. "That's what the sheriff assumed," she said. "But he is incorrect. I cannot tell you why, though, so please do not ask. This is a criminal investigation and I am under obligation to reveal my findings to no one outside the case."

Her gaze went from Jimmy to three people entering the restaurant—a couple in their late forties and a young man, early twenties perhaps. They went straight to a table in the front corner of the room as if it were reserved for them. Perhaps it was. The waitress brought them a tray of drinks, spoke briefly as if getting their usual order, then left.

The only other thing noteworthy about the new party was the young man with the couple, what looked like his parents.

It was the pasty white faced young man from the jury.

Rebekah cut one of her dumplings in half. "Jimmy, without drawing attention, I would like you to look at the family seated near the door, in the corner. Do you know who they are?"

Jimmy put his napkin to his mouth and turned his head, coughing lightly. He lowered it, looking back at her.

"Yes ma'am, those are the Monahans. Rich family. The son, Wilson, he's supposed to be some kind of smart. Going off to college in the east this fall."

She smiled, somehow not surprised Jimmy knew so much. "Well, if you aren't the man about town after only one day here."

Jimmy's eyes widened. "Did I do something wrong? That Deputy Wallace told me about them. Guess I shouldn't have been listening to gossip, but it sounded more like facts than gossip, and I don't know. God just seems to have me in places where I hear things I need to hear."

The waitress came and offered dessert. Rebekah declined but ordered a slice of apple pie for Jimmy.

He grinned in appreciation. "I sure hope I can pay you back for all of this, Miss Rebekah."

"You are, Jimmy." She glanced at the Monahans again. "This is very important work, and I must do it to the best of my ability. Will you trust me, Just Jimmy?"

"Sure, Miss Rebekah, I trust you. What do you want me to do?"

"I'm leaving early tomorrow morning to see Frances before I finish the autopsy. I would like you to keep an eye on things here, especially Wilson Monahan."

"What's special about him?" Jimmy asked.

"He wasn't upset at the trial today."

Jimmy looked at her like she'd lost her wits. But then grinned. "You're smart, Miss Rebekah. And you can count on me."

CHAPTER 4

A thump downstairs in the three-story mansion alerted Grace Palmer that her husband, Owen, was coming in late again. It was past 11 p.m.

Was he returning from yet another one of his secret meetings with Harold Monahan? Those two were always conspiring, even at this time, while she suffered in a state of shock over her daughter's death.

Owen hadn't allowed Grace to go to the trial, telling her to stay locked away in the house until it was all over. She never questioned his decisions, never questioned him like she should. Never checked on where he was when he wasn't lying in bed beside her.

The bedroom door opened; she pulled the comforter higher to shield her eyes from the lamplight in the hallway. The door clicked closed and she heard a match being struck.

The glare of lamplight hit her in the eyes as Owen lit the lamp on his side of the bed. He could see her eyes were open. She wished she'd shut them to at least pretend she was asleep.

Owen started removing his jacket. "We've decided to have Ruby's funeral in the morning."

Grace twisted the comforter around her hand into a fist,

refusing to look at him. He hadn't asked if she was ready to lay her daughter to rest, hadn't asked what kind of arrangements she wanted nor even where Ruby would be buried.

But she knew. Appearances were very important to Owen, so he would put Ruby in his family's plot at the cemetery. Grace was too worthless to have any say in the matter.

He continued talking as he removed his cufflinks. "We could have had that bandit hung today, and her resting in peace. That meddling woman doctor has upset the whole town."

Grace finally got the nerve to raise her eyes enough to look straight at him. Owen stared back, his eyes darkening.

"You think I killed her, don't you?" he said flatly.

Grace swallowed, fear for her own life paralyzing her, just as it always did.

Owen Palmer was a powerful man. There was no breaking loose from his physical or mental grasp.

He unbuttoned his shirt. "We're burying her tomorrow. She'll be out of my life once and for all."

He tossed his shirt aside and grabbed the comforter, yanking it away from Grace.

CHAPTER 5

Before dawn, Rebekah rented a buggy from the livery stable and set a good pace for the farm Deputy Biggins told her about, where Ruby's only female friend resided.

She had her medical bag with her as always in case she needed it, whether to treat someone or to reach for the pepperbox gun she kept in the false bottom.

The desert road was hard-packed and lonely, giving Rebekah a feel of isolation and hopelessness. But there was beauty in the desert too—decades-old cactus and dust-hearty reptiles that called the desert home. There was a sense of resilience and fight, one that renewed Rebekah's spirit and kept her company until the farm finally came into view of the early morning sun.

The place was unremarkable, simply a narrow one-story white house in sore need of a new coat of paint, a small barn, a water well, and a yard with chickens.

A man was at an ax grinding wheel near the barn, sharpening a blade, and there was a young woman in the sparse garden to the other side of the house. The couple was somehow surviving in the harsh desert.

Rebekah slowed the buggy and brought it to a halt near the

barn. The man, wearing trousers with suspenders over his long johns, looked up at her with his eyes barely showing under his shaggy blonde hair. He looked about as friendly as Pinto Diaz.

"What do you want, woman?" He sounded as friendly as Pinto, too.

Rebekah nodded toward the young woman still working in the garden, ignoring the new arrival. "I'm here to see Frances."

The man jerked his thumb toward the garden. "Don't stay long. She's got work to do."

Rebekah flipped the reins. "Thank you."

She maneuvered the buggy over to the garden where the young woman, who had seen Rebekah pull up, kept her back to her. "We ain't interested in whatever you're selling."

Rebekah set the brake and climbed out of the buggy, using the pole for the awning to keep her balance and her full skirt from catching on the wheel. "I would be a very poor salesman if I chose this route, wouldn't I?"

Frances didn't look up. From this angle, Rebekah could see her face was creased with tanned lines and freckles that made her older than her years. There was something else about her that made Rebekah think of Ruby, though she couldn't put a finger on it.

"I've come with news and to ask you something very important," Rebekah said, hoping the young woman would look up at her.

But Frances kept hoeing, her voice rough as if too much dust coated her throat. "I don't know anything worth driving out this way for. Not *anything* worth knowing that much."

"Not even that your friend Ruby is dead?"

Frances dropped her hoe and spun around, eyes and mouth wide. "Ruby's... dead?"

Rebekah reached out to take Frances' hand to comfort her, but the young woman jerked back, staring at the dirt.

"She was murdered," Rebekah said. "I'm sorry."

She expected Frances to burst into tears. But her shocked expression turned to one of peace.

"So, she got out after all," Frances murmured.

"What do you mean?"

Frances blinked and seemed to see Rebekah for the first time. Then it was like a curtain fell over her face, hiding her true emotions.

"Nothing."

"Frances, do you know Wilson Monahan? Did Ruby? Were they close?"

Frances frowned. "I don't recall that those two were all that friendly. Maybe."

Her eyes narrowed and her lip curled up at one end. Almost a snarl. "How's Owen Palmer taking it?"

Rebekah recalled the big man standing threat over her in the courtroom. "He's angry."

Frances snorted. "I'll bet."

She picked up her hoe and held it clenched in both hands. "Ruby was going to leave with me, going to find somewhere to live, but she got pulled back into that house. Figured she'd never git out, not since her ma moved them when Owen and her got hitched two years ago. Made Ruby take the name Palmer and everything."

Frances whacked the soil, then looked up to glare at Rebekah. "Lady, let me tell you something that *is* worth knowing—the Palmer's is one dark, dark house."

❧

THE RENTED HORSE moved at a slower pace on the return to town, or so it seemed to Rebekah. She wasn't sure if she was in a greater or less hurry to get back to the autopsy after her talk with Frances.

Her initial gut instinct had been correct. There was more to this case than a drunken bandit randomly murdering a girl in the town.

But why was Rebekah getting so involved, like Jimmy asked? She was a doctor, not a detective, nor someone who put aside her life to pursue justice in a matter that hardly involved her.

Yet there was something about the situation that she couldn't let alone. She had started the autopsy and she now had nearly the whole truth. There was one last aspect to the autopsy that could make all the pieces come together.

Her mentor never let up until he presented every piece of evidence possible for a criminal case. He taught her to do the same.

After what Frances hinted at with Owen Palmer, Rebekah needed to finish the autopsy. Then she would be ready to...to what?

Tell the sheriff what had really happened in Ruby's tragic life? He, nor anyone in that town, seemed inclined to know the truth.

But she would give the information to Deputy Thad Biggins. Whatever he chose to do with it, he could do. Rebekah would move on to her next assignment.

Only she didn't have one. Doctor McKinnon wanted her to return to the ranch and rest.

But Rebekah wasn't ready to go back.

The buggy jerked over a cactus growing in the unused road and Rebekah felt something give. She pulled the horse to a halt and climbed down from the buggy. She examined the front right wheel. It was loose.

The sun was moving faster now, the morning well underway. Rebekah needed to get back to town and finish the autopsy. But she wouldn't make it back with a loose wheel and there were no tools in the buggy.

How did a good buggy wheel like this get loose?

Rebekah glanced around the open desert road. No one in sight, but she felt a chill. Was Sancho Guerra out there somewhere, looking to break Pinto out of jail? What would he do if he happened upon her?

She didn't need to wonder what the answer was to that.

Rebekah pulled her medical bag out from under the bench seat and opened it. She freed the false bottom and retrieved her pepperbox, then snugged it in the waist of her skirt. It was just barely concealed when she fluffed her tucked shirtwaist over the butt.

There was nothing for her to do but walk the horse and buggy back to Frances' place to get the wheel tightened.

The beauty of the desert brought her no comfort now.

CHAPTER 6

It was nearly 11 a.m. when Rebekah rolled back into town. Frances's husband had begrudgingly repaired the buggy wheel, muttering something about the fool blacksmith letting it get loose.

Late morning was an odd time to arrive somewhere. People were typically at their destination by this point, occupied with the day. That certainly seemed the case in Hagan. It looked deserted like when Rebekah and Jimmy first arrived there. But there wasn't even clutter around the saloon.

Rebekah drove the buggy to the livery at the far end of town. She spotted Jimmy through the large, open doors, saddling his horse. He turned at the sound of her approach and the worry lines aging his face relaxed.

He came out the doors and met her at the rail where she halted the buggy.

Jimmy tied her horse up, talking over his shoulder. "Was getting worried about you, Miss Rebekah. Everything alright?"

"Loose wheel." She shifted to pull her medical bag onto the seat, away from Jimmy's view as she placed her pepperbox in the bottom again.

"I shoulda gone with you," Jimmy said. "But I kept an eye on things while you were gone, like you asked me to. Got something you're not going to like."

Jimmy moved down to the horse's rump, putting his arm on it as though creating a wall, and beckoned Rebekah forward with one finger. She left the bag on the seat and climbed out of the buggy.

Jimmy leaned forward and whispered, "Doc, I tracked that Wilson Monahan like you wanted me to, and he met up with this mean-looking hombre. Took me a minute to recognize him, but then I realized it was Dirk Ferguson."

Jimmy paused, his eyes round. Rebekah raised an eyebrow. He frowned. "Don't you know who Dirk Ferguson is, ma'am? One of the fastest guns out of Texas. Seen him shoot down one of the top gun slicks when he was just a kid, right in Fort Worth, five or six years ago."

"You would have been quite young, Jimmy."

He shrugged, that sheepish grin on his face. "Well, maybe I heard about it and seen his picture later, then put it together like I was there. Anyway, that Dirk Ferguson gave me the willies. I was poking around the pickle barrel outside the general store when I seen Wilson Monahan talking to him outside the saloon. Then Dirk turned and looked right at me like he had eyes in the back of his head, so I got a pickle out and started eating it." He took a breath. "I put it on your tab at the general store. Hope you don't mind."

"I didn't know I had a tab there."

"Oh." Jimmy's eyebrows scrunched together. "Well, you do now. I figured that was part of my assistant pay? If not, I'll get you paid back right away, Doc Beck."

Rebekah smiled. "Of course it's part of your pay, Jimmy. What else did you see? Where is everyone in town?"

Jimmy frowned. "That's the part you're not gonna like. That stepfather, Owen Palmer, he got up a funeral party this morning.

The undertaker came for the body at the ice house. Deputy Biggins didn't want to let him take it, but the sheriff overruled him. Funeral's going on right now."

⚜

THE CEMETERY SAT on a hill outside of town, a bare spot with a black, wrought iron fence surrounding it. Huge iron gates stood sentry as if warning anyone approaching that they needed permission to enter.

Rebekah drove the buggy at a fast clip to the open gates and halted. She handed the reins off to Jimmy for him to set the brake and secure the horse. There wasn't a moment to lose.

But never in her life as a physician did she imagine having to stop a funeral service.

She hurried through the gate and toward the back corner where everyone in town was gathered around an open grave. The scene was quiet, everyone with their heads bowed in silent respect.

Rebekah skimmed around the edge of the crowd, aiming for the sheriff. She also noted where Judge Slater was.

She halted slightly behind Sheriff Eden and Deputy Thad Biggins where they stood near the head of the grave. She would wait until the prayerful moment ended, then she needed to prevent dirt from being thrown on the casket with the five shovels stuck in the dirt pile next to the open grave. The sheriff or the judge had the power to make that call.

Head bowed, Sheriff Barney Eden didn't notice her. Deputy Biggins did. His head came up as he glanced back at her, his lips pulled in a tight line on his solemn face.

Jimmy came up beside Rebekah, trying to be easy but his foot kicked a rock. It skittered into the grave and landed on the pine casket with a thud.

Sheriff Eden raised his head and he glanced back, his expression one of disdain. A few more heads came up, a ripple effect until everyone was looking up.

Rebekah and Jimmy had unintentionally broken the moment of silence.

The time of laying someone to rest should be a respectful and peaceful one, when people contemplated the life of the deceased and their own destiny when their mortal life was over. This was what Rebekah's father taught her.

But it wasn't the time for it yet with Ruby Palmer. Rebekah spoke to the sheriff in a graveside tone, but one that could be heard by others closest to them.

"Sheriff Eden, I have not released this body for burial yet," she said. "There is more evidence I need to examine."

That got Owen Palmer's attention. He stood across the grave from her, his eyes two balls of fire. "I won't have you desecrating her body anymore! We are laying her to rest in peace. This is over."

The woman next to Palmer wore a black veil, her face a mess of tears. This was Ruby's mother, and Rebekah was certain her cheek was swollen from more than sobbing.

Rebekah spoke to Palmer, watching the judge from the corner of her eye.

"I understand you are distraught, Mr. Palmer. But a story cannot end until it's been told fully." She shifted to address the judge. "Judge Slater, I ask you to have this body returned to the doctor's office for me to complete the autopsy." She added three words with the best chance of convincing him. "For the records."

The judge's mostly bald head was exposed to the sun as the breeze stood his wisp of white hair up. He looked between Palmer, the sheriff, and Rebekah.

He muttered something that sounded like, "I really should."

The man on Palmer's left was Wilson Monahan's father and he looked as if he was about to go into a fit of rage. His son stood behind him, almost completely hidden from view of the grave. She didn't see Dirk Ferguson in the gathering.

Mr. Monahan pointed a finger at Rebekah. "You! That bandit would be picked clean by buzzards by now if not for you. This poor girl's soul will not rest in peace until then. But we can give her family some peace."

Monahan grabbed one of the shovels stuck in the dirt by the grave and scooped an enormous load. He flung it onto the wood casket. It landed hollow, the grave echoing a plea for truth and justice.

Owen Palmer took up another shovel and set to work. Rebekah suspected it was the most manual labor these two leading citizens had done in a while.

Mr. Monahan glanced up, glaring at his son. The younger man, looking as though he were about to faint, slowly took another shovel and joined them. Sheriff Eden strode around the grave and took up yet another.

The men worked feverishly to fill the grave. Rebekah watched, aware of Deputy Biggins observing her as if hoping she would say something else.

But there was nothing left that she could do, only testify what she did know at Pinto's trial. If it was even continued.

Rebekah went back to the buggy, letting Jimmy help her in. She was suddenly exhausted. He picked up the reins and flicked them, turning the buggy for the road down the hill.

They were partway to the bottom when a shot sounded. It came from the jail.

A second shot rang out as Jimmy pulled the horse to a quick stop and drew his six-gun. Rebekah instinctively reached for her medical bag as she glanced back to see that the town's people had also heard the violent echoes.

Sheriff Eden came running down the hill, followed closely by Deputy Biggins. Everyone else stayed frozen.

The lawmen rushed past the buggy. Rebekah freed her

pepperbox and turned forward again to see a lumbering figure stagger out of the jail and limp to a horse tied to the rail in front of it.

Pinto Diaz.

The bandit pulled himself up and kicked the horse before he was fully seated, charging out of town to the beat of the lawmen's gunfire.

CHAPTER 7

Rebekah spent the day in the doctor's office, treating patients. Few trusted an outsider—and a woman at that —enough to come to her. But nagging pain from a toothache and an accident drove three patients to her in desperation.

The distractions were welcome for Rebekah as the town waited tense for news of Pinto's recapture or death.

After the big man rode away, the sheriff discovered Deputy Wallace dead inside the jail, his back broken. He'd been able to get off a few shots before the bandit grabbed him fully.

That was all Rebekah could tell in the short time she had over the body before the sheriff shouted for her to get out. He and Deputy Biggins didn't bother raising a posse but immediately rode after the bandit.

The thing that caught Rebekah's attention was that Sancho Guerra hadn't been a part of the escape. Maybe he was dead somewhere, or already back in Mexico. Both thoughts comforted her.

The judge informed her that she would not do an autopsy on

Deputy Wallace. There would be no investigation into his death, and no mercy for the bandit when he was caught.

That was why she was surprised the next day to see Sheriff Eden and Deputy Biggins ride back into town in that odd late morning hour with a living Pinto Diaz in tow.

Rebekah stood on the porch of the doctor's office and shaded her eyes against the noon sun, same as several town people who stood stock silent as Sheriff Eden rode point with Deputy Biggins behind him, leading the horse Pinto had escaped on.

Pinto was laid forward on the horse's neck, his hands tied behind him. His right pant leg was soaked with his own blood. Rebekah couldn't see his face, but he was alive, barely holding himself in the saddle. It took a great deal to kill a man like Pinto Diaz.

While Deputy Biggins tied his horse and Pinto's up to the hitching rail in front of the jail, Sheriff Eden swung his horse around and addressed the loose crowd making a half-circle around him. They weren't lynch mob feverish. Even injured, Pinto was intimidating.

The sheriff's voice was gravelly, his vest splattered with blood.

"We'll finish the trial, right and proper," he said. His gaze skimmed over Rebekah, disregarding her as he continued to speak to his audience. "You have my word that this bandit will hang twice for what he's done in our town."

Eden swung off his horse and helped Deputy Biggins drag the bandit into the jail. Once Pinto was out of sight, the mesmerized crowd dispersed quietly.

Rebekah could tell they were worn out, worn out from days of being whipped into a frenzy that ended with a funeral, and now another death to grieve.

IT WAS time for the noon meal, and Rebekah started to lock the medicine cabinet with the key that Deputy Biggins had left her. A soft tapping on the office door halted her.

Jimmy, who'd been sitting on the table that served as the doctor's desk, swinging his legs, glanced at her and she nodded. There were no regular office hours for a doctor in the west.

Jimmy shoved himself off the table with his hands and strode to the door. He opened it to reveal Deputy Biggins on the other side.

The deputy nodded to Jimmy, then swept his hat off before addressing Rebekah. "The judge sent me, señorita, something about the records, you know. He asks for you to clean up Pinto before the trial this afternoon."

The judge's obsession with the records was humorous, but nobody smiled. Jimmy fairly well exploded.

"Hey now, that judge can't expect Doc Beck to get close to that mad bull! He would've killed her even when he thought she was a nun. What do you think he'd do now..."

While Jimmy railed, Rebekah opened the medicine cabinet and added what she might need to her medical bag. Having the pepperbox hidden in the false bottom didn't bring much comfort at the thought of being in Pinto's presence, but she was a doctor and difficult patients were a part of her profession. Pinto did take that difficulty to an extreme, though.

Rebekah turned with her bag and Jimmy squared his shoulders. "Well, I'm going with you. Ain't having you face him without protection."

Rebekah patted his arm as she passed, motioning with her bag for Deputy Biggins to lead the way. "Jimmy, you take such good care of me, truly. But I fear you would cause more harm than good. Pinto hasn't seen you yet and that could really turn him into a raging bull. Please go to the hotel restaurant. I will meet you there later."

They were all on the porch now, Jimmy's shoulders sagging.

Deputy Biggins said, "I will see that no harm comes to the doctor."

Jimmy didn't look convinced, but he let them leave. Rebekah knew he wouldn't be far away. She needed that thought before coming into close contact with Pinto Diaz. She remembered his ferocity when he and the bandits with him stopped her cart before she entered the mission.

This time, she wasn't wearing a nun's habit.

Deputy Biggins didn't say a word as they walked to the jail. He seemed tired, even more so than when she first met him, anxious as he came to the depot near Zapata to find her. She wondered when he last had a full night's sleep.

They entered the jail to find Sheriff Eden leaned back in his chair, shotgun crossed in his arms. He glared wordlessly at Rebekah. It certainly wasn't his idea for her to treat this prisoner.

Deputy Biggins unlocked the door straight across from the front door and opened it. Putrid fumes assaulted Rebekah. Sweat, unwashed body, and blood mixed with dust were a potent combination.

It wasn't unlike anything Rebekah had smelled before, but in the tightness of the two-cell jail, it was overpowering. A lady with delicate sensibilities would faint dead away.

Rebekah had grown into a lady according to her teachers, but life hadn't always allowed her to be delicate. She pushed forward.

A short hallway ran in front of the two cells. The first cell sat empty. Pinto Diaz occupied the second.

He lay on his side on the single cot, one arm hanging to the floor, the other bent back over his face at an awkward angle. After a few seconds, his shoulders raised with a breath. Even on the cot, he seemed to take up the whole room.

Deputy Biggins rattled the key in the lock and said in Spanish, "Diaz, the doctor is here to treat you. If you give her any trouble, I will shoot you dead."

A kind of rambling, muttered groan emitted from the bandit.

Deputy Biggins drew his pistol, swung the door open, and stepped inside. He positioned himself in the back corner where he would have a clear shot at Pinto even while Rebekah treated him.

Rebekah moved into the cell, its cracked adobe walls showing its age. She often found herself in dirty cells to treat prisoners— not something her father imagined when she went off to medical school. Her place was on the Omaha reservation, even with him gone now.

Rebekah set her bag on the floor and assessed the big man, wondering where to begin. His arm covered his face, but his leg wound was exposed to her, wrapped with a dirty bandana.

She began untying it as she spoke to Pinto in Spanish. "You will feel some pain as this loosens and also when I clean it. I advise you not to strike out. Deputy Biggins has his gun cocked. It would be impossible for him to miss at this range."

The bandage came loose and Pinto growled, flopping his arm back away from his face. Rebekah froze, staring at his face. Or what was left of it.

He was unrecognizable for the cuts, bruises, and swelling. It looked like she might have to remove his left eye.

Rebekah swallowed and looked up at Deputy Biggins. His eyes were awash with warring emotions. "Sheriff Eden said Pinto was resisting arrest. That is mostly true, señorita."

Rebekah didn't respond. They both knew the sheriff was already quick-tempered. The sight of the old deputy's body crumpled on the floor of this very cell pushed him outside the bounds of his oath.

Pinto squinted at Rebekah with his good eye. He muttered something in Spanish, his words sluggish on his swollen lips. She couldn't discern what he was saying but was fairly certain he was cursing her again.

Rebekah tore his pant leg away from the wound. The bullet was still in his leg.

She reached for her bag as she said to Deputy Biggins, "I'm going to put him out with chloroform. It will be too painful for me to remove the bullet otherwise."

Deputy Biggins shifted his feet, the emotions of anger, sorrow, and regret tracking across his face. "Should you bother, señorita? They will hang him tomorrow morning. Judge Slater only wants the bleeding stopped and him cleaned up."

Rebekah removed the bottle of chloroform and a clean cloth from her bag. Though she felt her kindness was wasted on the likes of Pinto Diaz, Doctor McKinnon showed her what true mercy was in the stories that came from his former patients. She could do no less.

She shifted on the stool to look up at Deputy Biggins. "Be that as it may, I am a doctor. My oath is to treat patients to the best of my ability, regardless of their potential lifespan."

Rebekah pressed the cloth to the end of the chloroform bottle, turned it up, then back. The next part was going to be tricky. She shifted so that her hand with a cloth was hidden from Pinto's view. He stared at the ceiling with his one good eye.

She spoke in Spanish. "Señor Diaz, I am going to put you under so that I can operate on your leg. Please be still."

She wasn't certain she'd said it correctly, but he got the gist and jerked his arm up as though to strike her.

Deputy Biggins moved in, uncocking the hammer of his pistol and raising it over the bandit's head where he could see it.

Pinto understood the gesture and stopped moving, his eye piercing Rebekah. If it had been a knife, she would be dead.

Rebekah covered his bloody nose and mouth with the chloroform. In moments, Pinto's breathing evened out as he stopped struggling against the pain of his body. This would also make it easier to do what she needed to do on his face as well.

Deputy Biggins moved back, holstering his gun and leaning against the wall. "Wish we had chloroform always for prisoners. It would save us all grief."

Rebekah moved down to Pinto's leg again. She was comfortable with conversation or with silence whenever she worked. But this was an opportunity to ask Deputy Biggins questions that still swirled in her mind about the case. She needed to decide if she trusted Thad Biggins.

The door between the cells and the sheriff's office was open, so she spoke in a soft tone as she began laying out her tools to remove the bullet. "Do you mind if I ask how long you have been a deputy under Sheriff Eden?"

Biggins matched her quiet tone. "I have been a deputy four years. The past six months, under Sheriff Eden."

Rebekah glanced up at him as she finished laying out her tools. "It seems you would be made sheriff after those years of service. You and Sheriff Eden seem about the same age."

Deputy Biggins' gaze went to the cell door behind her. "There are those in this town that do not care for overly straight shooters."

"And that left you out?"

The deputy didn't reply and Rebekah began sterilizing her scalpel. "Among those would be Mr. Monahan, and Owen Palmer, yes?"

"I do not suppose I have anything to say about them, señorita."

Rebekah cleaned the wound while she continued with, "May I ask if you have anything to say about Ruby Palmer?"

Rebekah looked up at him when she said the young woman's name. Thad Biggins didn't move, but she could see the change in his eyes, going gentle and sad. He stared at the bleeding leg wound.

"I suppose you may. I was in love with Ruby. She had much life and potential."

"But?"

Rebekah focused on the operation now, allowing Deputy

Biggins to take his time answering—if he would. She heard him sigh deep.

"As much as my heart was on her, I knew she was too loose to make a wife. But I hoped that if she were courted by the kind of man who treated her with care and respect as a lady should be treated, she would become one. I think maybe she was starting to. She settled down and we courted awhile. I was preparing to ask her to marry me when..."

Rebekah didn't look up, intent on her work. Deputy Biggins' voice was quiet and soft.

"I am not the kind of man she is accustomed to. Not the kind she wanted. I told her that God would want us to do things properly, in the way that I was raised, but she became very, very angry. She spurned me and returned to her ways." He sighed, a sound deep in his soul. "I thought we would be forever. You understand, yes? Now she is in that grave up on the hill and I'm here. I do not know why or what to do now, except see the man who killed her brought to justice."

Time passed slowly after that as Rebekah finished removing the bullet and stitching the wound. She wrapped it in a clean bandage, though there was nothing she could do about the blood-soaked pant leg. The sheriff needed to get Pinto new trousers and a shirt if he wanted to meet the judge's demand of having a clean prisoner in place for the remainder of the sham trial.

Rebekah moved to Pinto's face. She'd never seen one so damaged by a pistol-whipping.

It took an hour, and she was aware of Jimmy's voice in the sheriff's office. Hopefully, he had already eaten and was there to see about her. The sun was bright outside the bar-covered cell window, telling her it was only a short time until the trial. She might miss the meal herself.

She managed to save Pinto's eyeball and covered the repaired eye with a patch from her medical bag.

He was still unconscious, breathing slow. He was as ready for his hanging as she could make him.

Rebekah began cleaning her instruments. Thad Biggins was leaned against the wall and she said to him, "Deputy Biggins, you went through a good deal of trouble to bring me from Zapata. Neither the judge nor the sheriff felt an autopsy was necessary, but you did. Why?"

Deputy Biggins shifted away from the wall and squatted to hold her bag open wide as she began repacking it.

"I'm not sure, señorita. Just felt I needed to."

"Do you always live by your feelings, Deputy Biggins?"

He looked her in the eye. "Only when I feel those feelings are from God. You understand?"

Rebekah had once thought she did. She glanced over at Pinto. "You don't believe he's guilty, do you?" she asked.

Deputy Biggins said nothing, and Rebekah snapped her bag closed. She knew Pinto wasn't guilty. She just couldn't prove it was the man she suspected it was.

CHAPTER 8

Out in the sheriff's office again, Rebekah spotted Jimmy sitting in a chair by the wall, a plate in his lap covered with a red and white checkered napkin.

He sprang up, almost dumping the plate. "I brought you some food, Doc Beck. Hotel restaurant was about to close for the trial when they ran me out."

"Thank you, Jimmy. That was very thoughtful."

She turned to Sheriff Eden, who didn't look as though he had moved from his position with the shotgun crossed in his arms. He looked every bit as hostile as when she arrived, especially with his blood-splattered vest. Pinto's blood.

"Sheriff Eden, I will be at the saloon shortly to testify," she said. "But as long as you are trying Pinto Diaz for the murder of Ruby Palmer, you may inform Judge Slater that the charge should be upgraded to a double murder."

The sheriff curled his lip in a sneer. "You get too technical, Doc. Everybody knows Diaz murdered Deputy Wallace."

Rebekah shifted to where she could keep Deputy Biggins in her line of sight as she said, "I wasn't referring to Deputy Wallace. I was speaking of the child Ruby carried when she was murdered."

Deputy Biggins rocked back on his heels, his mouth agape. He was as shocked as she suspected he would be.

The sheriff wasn't. He slowly stood and dropped the shotgun on the desk with a clatter. He looked between Rebekah and Deputy Biggins, then balled his fists and planted them on the desk. He leaned toward Rebekah.

"I guess there's no need in the whole town knowing that," he said low, conspiratorial. "The family's been through enough. You keep shut, you hear?"

The sheriff was a puppet and she knew who was pulling the strings. After her visit with Frances, she suspected why.

Rebekah was once railroaded, and she wouldn't be again. She squared her shoulders, looking at the man far too weak to hold the weight of his office. "Sheriff Eden, I'll be under oath to tell the truth, the whole truth, and nothing but the truth—unless Judge Slater changes it to say only the truth that men like Owen Palmer will allow. I'll see you in court shortly."

Rebekah pivoted and headed for the door. Jimmy quickly opened it, balancing her plate in his other hand. Rebekah went through and didn't stop until she crossed the street and made it to the bottom steps of the doctor's office that led to the second floor.

She took a shaky breath, rubbing her temple. Jimmy caught up to her and offered her the covered plate as he asked, "What do you think, Miss Rebekah? You reckon the sheriff killed her?"

She accepted the plate. "You're very observant, Jimmy, but it's another man we're after. Or would be after if we were the ones investigating this case. But as you pointed out, we are not, and there's no reason to be involved further. Pinto Diaz will hang for murdering the deputy and, if Owen Palmer has his way, the murder of Ruby Palmer."

Rebekah headed up the stairs, not wanting Jimmy to see how disturbed she was. It wasn't the first time she witnessed the guilty go free, but there was no reason for her to be emotionally involved in this case.

Except Deputy Biggins' story haunted her. Ruby Palmer had been more than a body on her table to dissect. There was at least one person connected to Ruby's life who would live with the scars of what happened for the rest of his years.

⁂

REBEKAH ENTERED HER UPSTAIRS QUARTERS, ate quickly, then cleaned up for the saloon trial.

She still cared about her physical appearance at the court, though perhaps not as much. This was beyond what her autopsy mentor normally did in a trial, but he did tell her stories of facing a rigged jury when she was his assistant. He never backed down from telling the truth.

Rebekah crossed the street to the saloon with Jimmy. The same crowd was there, the atmosphere crackling with tension. But she had no trouble getting through.

The crowd parted, giving her looks that would have cut her down dead. Rebekah and Jimmy found a spot near the bar to observe the court proceedings about to get underway.

Sheriff Eden spotted her immediately from where he sat on one side of the shackled and somewhat cleaned up Pinto Diaz. Deputy Biggins sat on the other side and swung his head around to meet Rebekah's eyes. She nodded slightly at him. She would tell the truth and perhaps they would see justice served after all.

Her eyes went over the rest of the crowd and landed on the man who cornered her after the first day of the trial. He stared back at her, a smile on his lips that was both calm and a warning, like storm clouds in the distance flashing lightning long before the thunder sounded.

Jimmy leaned close to Rebekah's ear and whispered, "That's the gun slick I told you about, ma'am. Dirk Ferguson."

Judge Slater called the court to order and looked at the sheriff. "Well, Barney, are you going to get our next witness up here or not?"

As Rebekah recalled from the last time, she was the next witness. She shifted to begin making her way forward.

Sheriff Barney Eden stood quickly and addressed the judge. "Judge, we don't need any more witnesses. I have an affidavit here, with the autopsy report, signed by Doctor LaRoche. Ruby Palmer's neck was broken, and the size and strength of a man that it would take for that to happen fits Pinto Diaz to a T."

Deputy Biggins looked up sharply, then back at Rebekah, his eyes afire. They both knew Rebekah hadn't signed any sort of affidavit, nor was Ruby Palmer's neck broken. She was strangled.

Rebekah kept moving to the front of the room. "Your honor, that is a false document. I—"

Owen Palmer stood from his seat in the middle of the room in the rows to her right.

"George, it's time to end this," he barked. "Put the affidavit in your records and get on with sentencing Pinto Diaz for murdering my step-daughter."

Rebekah took note of the woman seated next to Owen Palmer, same as she'd been at his side at the funeral. The woman still dressed in black and wore a veil to cover her face. But Rebekah could see how she stared straight forward—her eyes blank. She resembled Ruby Palmer, not only in her blue eyes, blond hair, and hooked nose but in the look of death on her white face. Here was yet someone else who would bear the scars of Ruby's death for a lifetime. And someone who might know what really happened in the girl's life before she was killed.

Rebekah turned to appeal to Judge Slater one last time. "Your honor, if I will be allowed to testify..."

The judge banged his gavel, cutting her off. "You've said enough since you've been in this town. It's time you stop turning a bad situation worse. Deputy Biggins, take this woman out of here. Barney, give me that affidavit—for the records."

While Sheriff Eden strode to the bench with paper in hand, Deputy Biggins got to his feet and came to Rebekah's side. With the two lawmen parted, she could see Pinto's profile as he sat with his head hung, looking barely alive.

Was it the last time Rebekah would see him alive? Most likely, but that didn't matter so much to her as the real killer getting away.

Deputy Biggins came up to her and nodded toward the door.

Rebekah turned on her heel. "None of this is right, and you know it."

"I know it well, señorita."

Rebekah stepped out of the saloon, Jimmy and the deputy behind her. There was nothing more she could do, and nothing more she wanted to do. She was done with this town.

Once they were out on the porch, Jimmy must have read her thoughts because he asked, "We leaving now, Doc Beck? No sense in staying in a place you ain't welcome. I say it's time to shake the dust off our feet and light a shuck for Wyoming."

Though Rebekah could speak three languages fluently, she had trouble understanding Jimmy at times. She did get his general meaning and turned to Deputy Biggins.

"Jimmy is right." She looked Thad Biggins straight in the eyes. "I'm not sure there is a place in this town for someone who has honor and integrity."

Deputy Biggins didn't back down from her look, holding her gaze steady.

"I suppose, señorita, that a place with no honor and integrity is a place for a man who does have it, to stay."

His tone was sincere, yet it was hard to believe there were such men like Deputy Biggins in the world. Most of the seemingly upstanding men Rebekah had known were using integrity like the false front of a saloon.

But there had also been good men in her life that made her believe Deputy Biggins belonged in their category. She hoped she was right.

CHAPTER 9

There was a palpable blackness over the town as Deputy Thad Biggins walked his nighttime route, guarding the residents against other kinds of darkness. It was just past midnight, but he wasn't doing his route. He was taking a roundabout way to the doctor's office.

Thad placed his boot on the first step leading up to the second floor where Doctor Rebekah LaRoche was spending one last night in Hagan before leaving on the next morning's train.

The board was silent beneath his boot. He tested the next step. It creaked, so he skipped it and stepped onto the next one. And then the next.

He glanced back to make sure no one was sneaking around like him this night. Like the night Ruby was murdered.

One step at a time, Thad made his way to the top and the landing outside the door where Doc Beck was sleeping. He slipped his fingers into his vest pocket and withdrew the key that would fit the door. He had taken it off the ring earlier to avoid jingling now.

From the landing, he glanced around to check his limited view of the town again. No one was stirring, no one to see him slip the key into the lock.

Thad held the door tight to prevent it from making a popping sound as he turned the knob and slowly pushed the door open. There was no moon tonight to cast a shadow across the open floor space between himself and the bed on the far wall where Doc Beck was sound asleep.

He moved silently around the door and used both hands to close it quietly. He turned and took a step. The floorboard beneath him groaned.

Carefully, he removed his boots and left them by the door. He moved across the floor without a sound and came to stand over her.

Deputy Thad Biggins squatted, holding his holstered pistol to keep the leather from creaking. Then he reached toward the woman, one hand hovering above her shoulder while the other went toward her mouth. He moved them both at the same time, covering her mouth as he touched her shoulder.

CHAPTER 10

Rebekah was instantly aware of the hands on her as she came out of deep sleep. She jerked to free herself, but the hands held her fast.

A voice whispered, "Señorita Beck, it's me, Deputy Biggins. I need to speak with you."

Rebekah wasn't certain if she should relax or not. Strategically, it was the thing to do, so she softened her shoulders and neck. He removed his hands.

She rolled to her back, blanket pulled under her chin as she looked at the man crouching over her. He removed his hat and Rebekah saw tears in his eyes.

"Señorita, I must know," he said, his voice rough with the tears. "Why are you convinced Pinto Diaz didn't kill Ruby?"

Rebekah felt a shudder of relief go through her, a final decision that she could trust Thad Biggins. She sat up and the deputy scooted back so they could talk easier.

She held her open palms toward him. "I am going to place my hands on your throat like I'm choking you."

Deputy Biggins raised his eyebrows but didn't move. Rebekah put her hands around his neck above his bandana, evening whiskers pricking her hands. She squeezed lightly but pressed harder with her thumbs. He stared at her, intent on understanding what she was doing.

Rebekah loosened her grip as she said, "When I examined Ruby's body, I found she had been strangled. But it was by someone who could use their thumbs to cut off her wind." She pressed with her thumbs again. "Do you feel that? The bruises showed a left and right thumb did the deed."

Rebekah released his throat and dropped her hands. It only took a second for all confusion to leave Deputy Biggins' face.

His eyes lit up with the realization. "Pinto Diaz is missing his left thumb."

Rebekah nodded. "He and the men with him accosted me when I arrived at the mission. I could see his strength, the raw and untamed power in his body. But when he threatened me, I could see his left hand and the missing thumb. It matched the wanted poster description, so I knew who he was and how dangerous he was.

"When I saw him in the courtroom after my brief examination of Ruby Palmer, I knew he had not killed her. I began immediately to wonder who had and why, and who framed Pinto Diaz for it."

Deputy Biggins nodded, his eyes clear now. He looked ready to go out and drag the real killer through the streets, dead or alive. "Do you know who it was?"

Rebekah sighed. "I'm not certain, which is why I wanted to examine her body further. She was..." Rebekah halted, aware of the pain this would cause Thad Biggins. Ruby wasn't just a dead body to him.

But he was also a law enforcement officer, the only one in town that wanted the real killer brought to justice.

Rebekah went on. "She was abused and struck several times before she passed, but her cuts had already begun healing, at a rate that indicated the beating took place three to four hours before her death. My next step was to examine for older injuries. If there were any, such as a broken rib that hadn't healed properly, it could help us piece together what led to her death."

Deputy Biggins held her gaze steady. "We must have you finish that examination."

Rebekah wished she could do more to comfort him, to ease the desperation his pain caused him. "Be that as it may, Ruby has already been laid to rest."

Deputy Biggins swallowed, his tears coming back. "She is not resting, señorita, nor will she until we apprehend the real killer. I am willing if you are, Doc Beck."

The implications of what he was suggesting struck Rebekah like a wet slap across the face. She put a hand to her own throat.

"Deputy Biggins, I'm a doctor, not a grave robber."

Biggins put one hand on his knee, pressing hard, trying to regain control of his emotions. "Perhaps you do not need to see justice nearly as badly as I do, but I'm asking if you would be willing to finish the autopsy if I bring Ruby to you."

Rebekah rubbed her throat and pulled in a deep breath at the memory of Sancho Guerra with his hands around her throat, cutting off her wind.

She dropped her hand and swallowed, trying not to think about the details of robbing a fresh grave.

"I'm willing. And I will go with you."

❧

WHILE DEPUTY BIGGINS waited outside on the landing at the top of the stairs, Rebekah dressed quickly in the dark. It would upset anyone if they saw the grave being dug up, but could truly cause a fatal heart attack if they saw a woman standing nearby in a white nightgown.

Once dressed, she and the deputy went silently down the stairs in stocking feet.

At the bottom, Rebekah started pulling on her boots but felt a presence behind her. She whirled to find Jimmy creeping up to her, fully dressed and wide-eyed.

He whispered, "Miss Rebekah, what are you doing?"

Rebekah put a finger to her lips. She agreed with Deputy Biggins, that they needed to be absolutely silent, using the darkness of the night to accomplish their mission to track down the killer.

Somehow, Rebekah wasn't surprised at Jimmy's sudden appearance. She suspected he hadn't been sleeping all night in the hotel room she'd gotten for him, opting instead to sleep with his horse in the stable or prowling around at night, keeping an eye out for her. He was like an old guard dog whose primary life purpose was protecting his master. Considering what she'd been through the past few weeks, she didn't mind at all.

She and Jimmy followed Deputy Biggins through back alleyways, being careful to step just where he did to prevent disturbing crates and pallets stored behind buildings. Deputy Biggins seemed to know every board and box in their path.

While he had admitted his love for Ruby Palmer, Rebekah also knew he carried guilt that the murder took place under his watch. Of all the people he wanted to protect, he failed in the one person who meant the most to him.

Outside of town, they walked up the long road to the top of the hill where the cemetery was located. The iron gate shrieked in protest when Deputy Biggins opened one side. Rebekah instinctively looked back toward town. The wind was blowing in that direction and could carry the sound of the gate right to Sheriff Eden—or Owen Palmer. Could either of them truly sleep with their consciences tonight?

Rebekah went through the gate after the deputy, followed by Jimmy. Deputy Biggins took an extra moment to secure it from banging in the wind.

Though they were away from town somewhat, Jimmy held to

the oath they all seemed to have taken to remain as quiet as possible. He whispered in Rebekah's ear, "What exactly are we doing, Doc?"

Rebekah whispered back, "You likely don't want to know exactly, Just Jimmy."

Deputy Biggins led the way to the grave of Ruby Palmer. A shovel lay beside it. Deputy Biggins had already given this some thought and planning. He took up the shovel and began work.

Mouth gaping, Jimmy turned to Rebekah. She squeezed his arm, as much to reassure him they were doing the right thing as to assure herself. Would her father have understood the need for them to disturb a sacred place as he believed all graves were?

He would, same as he understood the things Rebekah did to the human body after death. Her father had loved and trusted her. How she missed that, and him, so very much. But there was nothing she could do to bring him out of his grave, nor even return home to visit it.

Rebekah blinked and turned from Ruby's grave to watch the town.

After several minutes, Jimmy reluctantly took a turn shoveling. He had that complete trust in Rebekah, too.

The night slid slowly by. Rebekah needed at least an hour to finish the autopsy, probably more. But digging up a grave was a slow process.

When Thad Biggins climbed out to give Jimmy another turn, she peered down, but could hardly see what the depth was of the black hole. She could barely make out the yellow of Jimmy's jacket after he hopped down and continued shoveling. When his shoulders disappeared into the hole, she heard him strike wood.

Ruby Palmer's casket.

Rebekah wondered if Thad Biggins was really prepared to exhume the body of the woman he loved.

She couldn't see his face as he climbed down into the grave next to Jimmy. Working together in the tight space, they cleared away loose dirt from the casket. They braced their feet against the side walls of the grave and Jimmy used the shovel to work the casket lid open. One more hard pull and the lid came up, bumping their legs. Jimmy gasped. Rebekah leaned over the grave and realized it was the smell gagging him.

Thad Biggins twisted and pulled himself out of the grave. Crawling out, he vomited to one side.

Rebekah wished she had Willow tea to settle the nausea all of them felt. But there was nothing she could do for Deputy Biggins' heart.

Jimmy scrambled out of the hole, taking several deep breaths. Rebekah put a comforting hand on his shoulder.

"I'm so sorry, Jimmy, but if you tie a bandana around your face, do you think you could carry the body back to the doctor's office? I must finish the autopsy."

Jimmy looked at her, aghast, as though she just asked him to rob his own mother's grave. Deputy Biggins turned on his knees and wiped his face with the back of his sleeve.

"I will carry her," he said, voice shaking.

Rebekah started to object. But this was Deputy Biggins' night, his mission, and she'd let him make his own decisions on what he felt capable of doing—no matter the scars it left on him.

The two young men tied bandanas over their faces and entered the grave again. Together, they lifted Ruby's blanket-clad body out of the casket and hefted it gently to the ground above.

Back out and on his feet, Deputy Biggins paused a moment. Then he scooped the body up in his arms.

Rebekah took another look toward town. The wind stirred the desert dust and spun a tumbleweed across the road to rest against the wall of the livery stable. No lights shown in town, no one prowling around.

No one knew a grave had just been robbed.

The trio made the trek back to the doctor's office, seeming to take twice as long as getting to the cemetery. Every squeak and creak had Jimmy jumping to look over his shoulder. Rebekah would have calmed him if she hadn't felt just as jittery.

But once inside the doctor's office, a peace came over her. It was time to finish the task she was trained for.

Rebekah directed Jimmy to cover the windows with spare blankets located in one of the cabinets. She didn't want light to shine from the inside and give away the clandestine operation. She started to ask him to crack the side window, but, much as she wanted fresh air, they couldn't chance the wind blowing the blanket and revealing a shaft of light.

While Jimmy covered the windows and Deputy Biggins situated the body on the exam table, Rebekah opened her medical bag that she had left in the office. She pulled out a small bottle of lavender oil, turned the tip over on her finger. She dabbed the drops on her upper lip.

Once the windows were covered, Rebekah lit a lamp and carried it behind the curtain of the exam room. She glanced back at Jimmy and Deputy Biggins, their faces pale and drawn.

"Please stand guard outside," she said. "I'd rather not end up behind Sheriff Eden's bars to stand trial before Judge George Slater in this town."

Jimmy started to leave but Deputy Biggins lingered.

"May I wait on the other side of the curtain, señorita? I want to know what you find as soon as you find it."

Rebekah handed him the bottle of lavender oil.

"You may. I'll let you know soon."

CHAPTER 11

Dirk Ferguson stood against the adobe wall of the blacksmith shop, one foot propped on it behind him and his thumbs hooked casually in his low-slung gun belt. In the darkness of early morning, he watched Willy pace back-and-forth, running his hands through his hair and yanking on it. His eyes were bloodshot and wild, and his hands hadn't stopped moving once.

Maybe Willy was remembering what it felt like to have his hands around Ruby Palmer's throat, choking her. He probably hadn't even felt what his hands were doing. He'd been out of his head, and he was mostly out of his head now. Dirk watched him close but didn't move.

"You better settle down, boy," Dirk said, his voice a low growl. "Your daddy wouldn't be happy with what you did tonight, going up to her grave."

Willy halted and, both hands about to pull his hair out from the roots, faced Dirk.

"What I did *tonight*?" Willy barely got the words out between gulping air. "It's what I did nights ago that is haunting me. But I needed to go there, needed to see her grave without all those people staring at me. They all know I did it. Everyone knows! That grave knows. It's there, wide open, empty, screaming at the world that I am a killer!"

Willy released his hair and dropped his hands to stare at them. He held them high for Dirk to see.

"Such small hands," Willy whispered. "How could I have taken her life with these hands and not even known it?"

Dirk wondered at this young man's quiet genius, how he could make it through an Ivy League preparatory school and now about to attend one of the most prestigious colleges in the United States. Just a boy from the hick town of Hagan, Willy was intelligent. Except for one insane moment when he took a girl's life.

But none of that mattered. Harold Monahan was paying Dirk to keep a lid on it until Pinto Diaz was hanged. That would end things in Willy's mind, and he'd be sent off to college. Dirk would head west with a hefty purse, maybe go to California.

There were only a few hours to go until dawn when Pinto Diaz would hang. But the wild look in Willy's eyes said he would go screaming down the street any second.

Dirk contemplated knocking him out and hog-tying him in the Monahan barn until it was over. But Willy might still go berserk after coming to. The best thing was to funnel the young man's guilt and panic in a violent direction.

"You listen to me, good," Dirk said. "I'll tell you what likely happened at the grave. That nosy Doc Beck and self-righteous Deputy Biggins dug it up. They think there's still something with Ruby's body that will lead them to the real killer. Only one thing to do: it's time to turn Ruby's body to ashes. Then there won't be no more fighting over it."

Willy's eyes popped. "What...what are you saying?"

"I'm saying the doctor's office is one of the newer wood frame buildings, not adobe like most buildings in town." Dirk rapped the adobe wall behind him for emphasis. He needed to ground

Willy in reality. "With the dry spell we've had, it'll go up in a heartbeat and to ashes in minutes."

Willy grabbed his own arms, squeezing tight with those hands of death. "But the fire could spread and burn some of the other buildings or catch roofs on fire. We could burn down the whole town!"

Dirk chuckled. "You got some kind of special love for this town?"

"But..." Willy's eyes darted around as if looking for a way to escape his own skin. "Those people might still be inside."

Dirk drilled him with a hard look. It was time to use the last threat he had against Willy. "Like I said before, you swing just as high for killing one as you do three."

Willy stilled. Until that point, he only thought of the guilty conscience he suffered for his moment of blind rage. The look on his face said he hadn't fully considered the fact that if he were found out, he'd hang instead of Pinto.

Dirk pushed away from the wall and gripped Willy's shoulder in a firm squeeze.

"Don't you worry, Wilson Monahan. I'll be right behind you."

CHAPTER 12

"Soon" was two hours later. Rebekah knew there wasn't much time left until dawn—and Pinto Diaz's hanging.

The man was guilty of murdering Deputy Wallace, although he hadn't stood trial for it. But if the town went through with hanging him, the truth about Ruby Palmer's killer would never be known.

Rebekah covered Ruby's body and stepped out from behind the curtain. Deputy Biggins was seated near the door. Hands caked with dirt from digging the grave rested on his trousers, his boots painted red from the clay.

He looked up at Rebekah expectantly. "Señorita?"

She halted, something coming through her nostrils beyond the smell of lavender and her work. She looked at Deputy Biggins. He seemed to realize it at the same time. He shot to his feet as the door flew open.

Jimmy stuck his head in. "Get out, Doc! The whole building's on fire!"

Rebekah started for her bag as she called to Jimmy, "Wake the sheriff, get a bucket brigade going!"

She collided with Deputy Biggins who was making a beeline for the exam table. Rebekah grabbed his arm.

"You can't take the body," she said firmly. "You must leave her. We've learned what we could."

Deputy Biggins' eyes were cloudy, confused, but he nodded. There was the sound of rattling, then the side window exploded.

Flames licked into the room, catching the blanket over the window on fire.

Rebekah and Deputy Biggins ran out through the door as the room filled with smoke behind them.

Jimmy's shouts had people running from buildings and houses on the side streets of the small town. Deputy Biggins made sure Rebekah was away from the building, then ran back, shouting for the general store owner to open up his warehouse so they could get to his supply of buckets.

Rebekah climbed the steps of the milliner shop across from the doctor's office and turned to face the burning building. There was nothing she could do but watch the men jostling to get in place for the fire brigade. There were more men than buckets.

She clung to her medical bag, thinking of her carpetbag in the upper floor of the doctor's office. The fire hadn't reached it but was spreading fast. Thankfully, she didn't travel with her most valued possessions, like the photograph of her parents. It was safely back at Doctor McKinnon's ranch.

As the flames licked up the side of the building despite the bucket brigade's efforts, Rebekah sensed someone coming up behind her.

She turned quickly to find the gunslinger, Dirk Ferguson, there in the shadows.

He smelled of whiskey, but he didn't look drunk as he leaned against a post supporting the porch. He cocked his head at her, offering an unnerving smile like he might give when facing another gunfighter, one he was about to kill.

"Looks like you got lucky, Doc," Dirk Ferguson said, his voice the same tone he used when warning her in the trial to stay away from the case. "Leaving on the train soon, ain't you, right after the hanging?"

It was an odd statement to make while everyone else fought a fire that threatened the entire town.

Rebekah didn't trust taking her eyes off him. "I do not see how my itinerary is your concern, Mr. Ferguson."

Dirk Ferguson cocked his head the other way. "You know my name. That's something, leastways."

He ambled off the porch and toward the bucket line. He joined in at a gap when one man stepped away, coughing. Ferguson took a turn grabbing buckets and swinging them to the next man in the line.

Jimmy was at the water spigot of a horse trough in front of the general store, his face red as he worked the hand pump. Another man relieved him when he stepped back, breathing hard.

Jimmy looked over toward Rebekah, and she nodded. They'd done their part in helping this town. Only God knew what would happen next.

❧

FOR HALF AN HOUR, the people of the town fought the fire. At one point, red embers jumped to the building beside the doctor's office, but two men had already climbed onto the roof with wet blankets and quickly put it out.

The activity slowed to a halt as the last flame was extinguished. A few men walked around with buckets, pouring water on the remaining coals.

The doctor's office was scarred but saved.

With the fire out, its brilliance no longer lighting the area, Rebekah realized the first streaks of gray dawn were coming over the town. It seemed everyone had the same realization. People exchanged looks, each wondering who would make the first move as if they alone would be responsible for setting the day in motion.

The whole town was there, gathered for the event they anticipated at dawn. Rebekah noted Owen Palmer among the crowd. Judging from the look in his eyes when they met hers, he didn't seem pleased she wasn't inside the doctor's office while it burned.

Someone finally made the first move. A voice shouted from the other side of the crowd, "All right, now that's over, we got a hanging to do!" The voice belonged to Dirk Ferguson. "This town's had nothing but trouble from Sancho Guerra's bandits, and it's time to hang one of them!"

The town, adrenaline exhausted, came alive again at the mention of the hanging. The people dropped the buckets to the ground, causing sporadic clanging to ring out, and started toward the jail.

Deputy Biggins darted through the people and jumped to the porch of the jail, grabbing a post to swing around and face the audience.

"There will not be a hanging this dawn!" He shouted. He licked his soot-covered lips and glanced toward Rebekah. "We have proof that Pinto Diaz did not kill Ruby Palmer. That means someone, someone right here, did."

A common gasp went through the spectators, and people exchanged shocked expressions.

Rebekah joined Deputy Biggins on the porch, Jimmy right behind her. She needed to take the kind of stand her father would have.

"That is correct," she said, her voice steadier than she thought it would be after being up nearly all night, robbing a grave, performing an autopsy, escaping a fire, and now facing a whole town set against her.

She pressed on. "I suspect the fire was set intentionally to erase the evidence of Ruby's body that is inside the doctor's office."

More gasps, and Dirk Ferguson stepped forward.

"I reckon she's right," he sneered, one hand on the butt of his gun as though that was its natural resting place. "Ruby's grave was dug up sometime last night."

He looked at Rebekah, his eyes alight with accusation. "I reckon this Doc Beck will stoop to anything to save Pinto Diaz. Must've been more going on in that mission than her being a hostage."

Jimmy darted out from behind Rebekah. She quickly put out a hand to halt him. Jimmy did have the sense to remember Dirk Ferguson was a professional killer who had never lost.

Jimmy glanced at Rebekah and settled with shouting, "That's a dirty lie! You ain't going to get by saying something like that about Doc Beck."

She said quietly to him, "It's all right, Jimmy. Ferguson is merely trying to distract from the truth. I believe he's been doing that all along."

Owen Palmer pushed his way to the front of the gathering, leaving his wife back a few rows, and said, "Let's just get the hanging over with! Barney, do your duty."

Sheriff Barney Eden had stayed in the background during the whole ordeal. Rebekah had seen the look of fear in his eyes during the fire as he stood back, pretending to supervise the operation while Thad Biggins actually did. The sheriff was only tough when facing a woman, or a wounded prisoner.

Now Sheriff Eden stepped onto the porch, heading for the door, but Deputy Biggins blocked his way.

Biggins said something to him quietly, but Eden's eyes glowed with contempt.

"Move it, Thad."

Deputy Biggins did not. He spoke for all to hear. "When I took an oath along with this badge, I meant the words I said. I will see justice done, even if it means a dirty killer like Pinto Diaz gets a fair trial and the real killer found guilty. That is why I brought Doctor LaRoche here."

Sheriff Eden's jaw twitched. "I reckon you wouldn't care so much if that bandit was a white man."

Rebekah found herself wanting to take a step closer to Thad Biggins, wishing she could ease the sting of pain on his face.

But he recovered on his own and said steadily, "White, Mexican, or half does not matter. We cannot run this town with being paid off by Monahan and Palmer every week."

Eden's neck reddened. Before Deputy Biggins could flinch, the sheriff drew his gun, cocked it, and aimed it at Biggins' midsection.

Rebekah gasped, putting one hand over her mouth, waiting for the shot to come. Mercifully, it didn't.

Deputy Biggins slowly spread his hands to the side, his eyes traveling up from the gun to meet the sheriff's. His eyes studied his opponent with a rare intensity from the gentle young man.

No one moved. Sheriff Eden didn't seem to know what to do next. Finally, he said from the side of his mouth, "Dirk and a few of you other men, get that killer out here and string him up."

In that moment, Rebekah knew Deputy Biggins could lose his life. Men—and women—lost their lives too easily in the west.

But that shouldn't stop someone from doing what was right.

Rebekah didn't know what gave her the courage to live that, but as Dirk Ferguson and two other men pushed toward the steps of the jail, she made her decision. She hoped Thad Biggins was ready.

As Dirk Ferguson passed by her, she stuck her foot out and tripped him. He stumbled to the boardwalk by Sheriff Eden.

At the same instant, Deputy Biggins grabbed the sheriff's wrist and shoved his gun arm downward. The gun went off, a puff of dust flying up from the floorboards by their feet.

Deputy Biggins swung back around with a right hook to catch the sheriff under the jaw, knocking him into the wall.

Dirk Ferguson was back on his feet, clawing for his gun.

Rebekah quickly undid the straps of her medical bag, going for her pepperbox, but she wouldn't be in time.

From beside her, Jimmy's six-gun was suddenly in his hand and spitting a fireball. His shot nicked Dirk Ferguson's hand just as Dirk was bringing his six-gun up to bear on Deputy Biggins. The gun went flying and hit the closed door of the jail.

The shot shocked Dirk Ferguson, who immediately gripped his hand, turning to try and locate who caught him so off guard. He stared at Jimmy, who kept his aim on the gunslinger.

No one looked more shocked than Jimmy, though Rebekah felt she could take the prize.

During the quick gunfight, Deputy Biggins managed to wrest Sheriff Eden's gun away. He jumped to the other side so he could cover the sheriff and Dirk Ferguson at the same time. A glance at Ferguson's bleeding gun hand told him that wasn't necessary.

Thad Biggins gulped and shouted, "All right, every one be still! The doctor has something she wants to say."

Rebekah took a shaky breath and another look at Jimmy, who was frozen. She didn't believe he'd blinked even once since outdrawing Dirk Ferguson.

Rebekah met Deputy Biggins' eyes, the emotions that raged there—love for Ruby, anger for the killer. If nothing else, she was doing this for Thad Biggins, the only respectable man with courage in the town of Hagan.

She stepped toward the center of the porch, taking note of where the key players were. Even Judge Slater was there. For the records, of course.

She zeroed in on the Palmers, now standing to one side of the crowd. She wished she could have spoken with Mrs. Palmer before this moment, but this was the time.

She said softly, but where everyone could hear, "You didn't know your daughter was pregnant when she was killed, did you?"

A ripple went through the crowd at the announcement. Owen

Palmer looked infuriated; Mrs. Palmer as though she were going to faint. She hadn't known about her grandchild.

This wasn't the sort of thing spoken about publicly, but justice hung in the balance, and Rebekah didn't know any other way it could be done.

Gathering her courage, Rebekah rounded to face the far edge of the crowd. Her gaze landed on the young man from the jury, the only one not of the same mind as the others ready to lynch Pinto Diaz.

She called out to him, "You killed her, didn't you, Wilson Monahan? You discovered she was with another man's child and strangled her in a blind rage."

The few people standing close to Wilson Monahan moved a step away, staring at him. He had the look of a man who was completely worn out from battling himself.

His breaths came in gasps. "No...no, the child was mine! But I didn't mean to kill her. She was threatening to blackmail me. I had school, my father..."

"The child wasn't yours, Mr. Monahan." Rebekah turned back to Owen Palmer. "It was yours, wasn't it, Mr. Palmer?"

If there had been any sparks left from the fire, it would have ignited the tension over the crowd. Owen Palmer was that spark. He exploded, "How could you possibly know about that..."

He looked like he was about to choke on his tongue when he realized his confession.

Rebekah relaxed her shoulders. "I didn't know for sure. But now we all do. I did know Ruby was beaten and abused, often, in the past two years. That is how long you and Mrs. Palmer have been married, or so Frances told me."

Something snapped in Mrs. Palmer's expression. She backed away from her husband. "I always knew." She coughed on her sudden tears and spittle. "I always, always knew. There were other girls, too, weren't there?"

To Rebekah's right, the hoarse, boyish voice of Wilson

Monahan said, "It's true. Ruby told me. I didn't believe her. I didn't even love her. It was only one night. She was going to ruin my life over one night."

Rebekah turned back to him. "It seems you ruined your own life over one night, Mr. Monahan."

Wilson buried his face in his hands, but Rebekah could still hear his wail. "Dirk was supposed to take care of everything! Even set fire to the building, trying to hide the evidence of Ruby's body. Dirk found us after I killed her, right after, you know."

Dirk Ferguson, still holding his bleeding hand and covered by two guns, growled, "Shut up, Willy."

Wilson raised his head and went on like he didn't hear a thing. "Dirk knew that bandit was hiding in the livery. Clonked him over the head and poured whiskey on him, made it look like he was drunk, and put Ruby's scarf in his hands. But it was my hands." Wilson held his hands high in the air. "These hands! Like the doctor said. They strangled Ruby."

Wilson's hands, stiff and claw-like, finally relaxed with his confession.

The gray dawn was turning into brilliant hues of purple, red, and yellow as the sun peeked over the new day. Rebekah wouldn't be surprised if it spotted the inner darkness of this town and scurried away, never to return. That was what she planned to do.

After a few seconds of silence, Judge Slater came slowly up the steps of the jail. At the top, he met Rebekah's eyes, looking apologetic. His stalk of white hair was speckled with ashes from the fire and quivered as he turned to face the crowd.

"I suppose it's better to hang the right man for the right murder than not," the judge said, sounding like he was mustering his courtroom voice, but failing miserably. "We'll try Pinto Diaz and hang him for the deputy's murder, and I reckon Wilson Monahan will get the same for killing Ruby. That is, if Doc Beck is willing to sign a new affidavit...for the records."

He looked over at her and she nodded. "Owen Palmer should

be charged as well," she said. "The final things I discovered on Ruby Palmer's body was evidence of the long-term abuse—fractured ribs and broken bones that healed without a doctor's care. I have a feeling I would find the same types of injuries on Mrs. Palmer. I believe she and Frances will testify."

Judge Slater shifted his jaw back and forth then straightened his spine for perhaps the first time in years.

He barked at Deputy Biggins, who still had the sheriff and Ferguson covered, "Thad, I hear-by appoint you sheriff. I reckon you know who all to arrest. You, boy, Jimmy, ain't it? I appoint you as temporary deputy. Give Sheriff Biggins a hand."

Jimmy, gun still out and cocked, raised his eyebrows and looked to Rebekah for permission.

She smiled. "Far be it for me to go against the judge's orders."

Jimmy grinned tentatively, and the newly appointed Sheriff Thad Biggins had him cover Eden as well as Ferguson while he proceeded to make the other arrests. Owen Palmer and Wilson Monahan didn't resist.

Thinking about the two-room jail had Rebekah wondering which of the three men would have the privilege of sharing a cell with Pinto Diaz.

CHAPTER 13

Since Wilson Monahan and Owen Palmer confessed fully to their crimes, Rebekah was able to sign an actual affidavit of her testimony from the autopsy of Ruby Palmer's body. The case was finished for her.

Before packing to leave town, she attended the real funeral for the girl, officiated by a minister, and a few kind words given by Sheriff Thad Biggins for the eulogy. It was a small gathering, but hopefully, the whole ordeal taught the town's people a few lessons. Not the least of which, that it was important who they pinned a tin star on.

After the funeral and everyone moved away, Rebekah joined Thad Biggins for the walk back. She decided to be blunt.

"This town does not deserve you, Sheriff Biggins," she said. "They were determined to throw truth and justice to the wind and even stampede over you when you tried to do what was right." She paused, thinking of those she'd known willing to do the same. Her father came to mind, along with a man at the McKinnon Ranch. "But I'm glad you're staying, despite it all."

"Everyone needs grace, ma'am."

Rebekah glanced up at him with a half-smile. "You remind me very much of another man I know."

"Is he a godly man?"

"Very much so."

"Then I'm honored."

Jimmy met them at the hotel porch, carpetbags on either side of him, her medical bag held tight under his arm. "Ready, Doc? I'm sure anxious to get to Wyoming."

Sheriff Biggins smiled at him, but there was a somber tinge to it. "I would think you are much ready to leave, Señor Jimmy. When word spreads that you outdrew Dirk Ferguson, there will be many challengers that search for you."

Jimmy gulped and Rebekah patted his arm. "Maybe in the older days, Jimmy. But tell me, how on earth did you learn to draw and fire so fast?"

He shrugged, his cheeks red. "Don't know, ma'am. Can't believe I did it. Never drew down on a man before, just sagebrush and tin cans. Time passes kinda slow when you're by yourself at a line cabin, I guess." He grinned at Sheriff Biggins. "And it's Just Jimmy."

The way he said it told Rebekah he felt he was beginning to feel the "just" part.

Jimmy squatted awkwardly and picked up the carpetbags, one on each side.

Rebekah looked at the bags then across the road to the partially burnt doctor's office. The town had already set about cleaning and repairing it. There could be more people who needed her before the town's doctor came back.

It wasn't her responsibility and the telegram she received from Doctor McKinnon that morning urged her to come to the ranch. It was time for her to take a break.

But she found herself grasping for excuses not to go. She was ready to leave this town, but Sheriff Biggins' gentle spirit reminded her of why she didn't want to go back, of the one man she didn't want to see, not quite yet.

She tugged her medical bag out from under Jimmy's arm. "I think I'll stay on until the doctor returns, Jimmy." She regretted his disappointed look, but at his age, it was nothing a slice of apple pie wouldn't fix.

She glanced at Thad Biggins. "If that's all right with you, Sheriff Biggins?"

He grinned and Rebekah knew his wounds would heal and leave a reminder of grace.

"We would be honored to have you, Señorita Doc Beck."

CHAPTER 14

On a butte a quarter of a mile away from the town, rising higher than the hill where the cemetery was, sat two men on horseback. They were positioned behind a rock formation that blocked them from view, yet they could see what was happening in the town, as they had for days now.

That day, they watched a funeral procession climb the hill, lay a body to rest, and the people return to their normal lives. But two figures lingered toward the back—one was a woman in a navy-blue skirt that cut a slender and attractive figure. Far more so than she had in the black and white nun's habit, her dark brown hair covered while she pretended to speak neither English nor Spanish well.

The woman had been clever in her deception, choosing to be a woman from a revered faith. It was something that Sancho Guerra was now grateful for. The unholy deception was the reason for the fire of anger in his son's eyes.

It was the kind of fire that could burn out of control and consume Edgardo, or the kind that could refine him and shape him into the kind of gentleman bandit Sancho envisioned his son becoming.

That refinement would begin with the act they were about to perform. It was one Edgardo plotted himself with such precision that Sancho couldn't imagine having done it better himself. There was only one issue—they couldn't implement the plan and save Pinto Diaz from hanging. But it was worth the life of his right-hand man for Sancho to see his son like this.

In an ironic twist, the woman doctor broke the link Edgardo had with his dead mother and her religion. Edgardo thought too much of the teachings his mother instilled in him against Sancho's wishes. Sancho was raised in the same faith and adhered to the basic rudiments of it, but his wife had taken it too far. She even criticized the way of life Sancho was rearing their son in, saying they would go to hell for stealing and killing.

Sancho didn't grieve her death.

And now, this woman doctor had destroyed the image of holiness for Edgardo and the religion he held sacred because of his mother. That opened Edgardo's grief afresh and offered Sancho the chance to finally and fully mold his son in his own image.

Edgardo sat still on his horse, which was stolen from a local ranch. Edgardo had shot the man who tried to stop them from stealing the fresh horses, wounding the ranch hand in the leg. It was the first time Edgardo shot anyone, and he'd done it in such a calm way that a thrill of pride went through Sancho.

Sancho now gestured to the cemetery on the hill below and across from them. "That was her, my son. The one the American newspapers hailed a hero; a sophisticated spitfire; someone beloved to celebrate."

Edgardo continued to sit stiffly, only his horse's ears flicking back to catch the deep tone of his voice. "She is a liar and deceiver who used the holy cross for her deception," Edgardo spat. "We will finish her."

Sancho smiled, shifting in his saddle to rest his forearm across the horn, half-turned to face his son. "Not we, my son. *You* will finish her. I am only here to guide you. You are capable of this."

Sancho paused, then spoke a simple but powerful phrase to his son for the first time. "I am proud of you."

Edgardo met his father's eyes and the fire of refinement flared in the direction Sancho wanted it. He would use this woman, this Doc Beck, to refine his son into a leader like Sancho Guerra himself.

Dearest reader,

Thank you for reading *Grave Robbers (Doc Beck Westerns Book 3)*. I truly hope it entertained and delighted you!

If you fell in love with the main characters, Rebekah, aka "Doc Beck," and Jimmy, you'll be excited to know **book 4, *Desert Captive***, is now available! You can order it on any major retail site or through www.SarahElisabethWrites.com.

I'd be thrilled if you took a moment to write your thoughts in the form of a review for *Grave Robbers* and post it on your favorite retail outlet and Goodreads. You'll help other readers find this series.

To discover more of my books, free short stories, and to generally stay in touch with me, I invite you to join my VIP reader newsletter. You'll receive a free copy of *The Executions*, book one in my historical fiction *Choctaw Tribune* Series. Please join me through:

www.subscribepage.com/sarahelisabethwrites_choctaw-tribune-book-one.

Speaking of history, the character of Doc Beck was inspired by Dr. Susan La Flesche (Omaha), who is hailed as the first American Indian to earn a medical degree. In continued research, my mother found Dr. Isabel Cobb (Cherokee), the first woman physician in Indian Territory, in very nearly the same years as Dr. La Flesche.

Lastly, if you're not familiar with my heritage books based on my Choctaw history and culture, you can check them out on www.SarahElisabethWrites.com. Questions? Please send them my way: me@sarahelisabethwrites.com

—Sarah Elisabeth Sawyer

Historical Fiction and Western author
Tribal member of the Choctaw Nation of Oklahoma

CANYON WAR (DOC BECK WESTERNS BOOK 1)

Traveling the West as a female physician, 34-year-old Doctor Rebekah LaRoche is no stranger to trouble. But on her way to New Mexico Territory, an unexpected stay in Amarillo, Texas, leads to confrontation with the Baxter clan – four brothers bred for trouble – and finds Rebekah in deep trouble.

Cattle rancher Clem Baxter's private war over grazing rights in the Palo Duro Canyon turns disastrous, and when the dust settles, one of the Baxter brothers is hurt bad. Clem sends for a doctor, not a woman, but that's what he gets when Rebekah, known as "Doc Beck," arrives at the ranch.

Now held at Clem's ranch against her will, Rebekah must plot to flee through the night with her young friend into the dangers and beauty of the Palo Duro Canyon.

Of Omaha Indian and French descent, Rebekah has always relied on her wits to get her out of any situation. But does that include facing down men willing to die—and kill—for a wild piece of land just as dangerous as any bullet?

Canyon War **is available on multiple retailer sites.**

♦♦♦

MISSION BANDITS (DOC BECK WESTERNS BOOK 2)

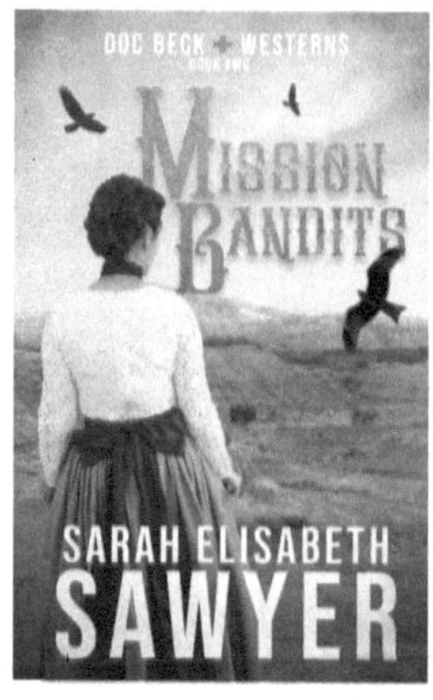

The Mexican army, a town marshal, and the Sancho Guerra gang are facing off when Doctor Rebekah LaRoche and her new friend, Jimmy, arrive in Zapata, New Mexico Territory. The bandits are holding hostages at Hope Academy, a school for girls located in an old mission outside of town, and Rebekah feels compelled to act—she was sent to the school to modernize the infirmary, not see the innocent occupants murdered.

The notorious and charismatic bandit, Sancho Guerra, led his band of men on a pillaging spree from Mexico to the mission and has proven his indifference to killing, prepared for any tricks the army or the Zapata town marshal throw at him.

But he isn't prepared for Rebekah, and now the Mexican army colonel wants her to do something terrifying—enter the mission and help with the capture of the deadliest men in the territory.

Mission Bandits is available on multiple retailer sites.

THE EXECUTIONS (CHOCTAW TRIBUNE SERIES, BOOK 1)

Who would show up for their own execution?

It's 1892, Indian Territory. A war is brewing in the Choctaw Nation as two political parties fight out issues of old and new ways. Caught in the middle is eighteen-year-old Ruth Ann, a Choctaw who doesn't want to see her family killed.

In a small but booming pre-statehood town, her mixed blood family owns a controversial newspaper, the *Choctaw Tribune*. Ruth Ann wants to help spread the word about critical issues but there is danger for a female reporter on all fronts—socially, politically, even physically.

But what is truly worth dying for? This quest leads Ruth Ann and her brother Matthew, the stubborn editor of the fledgling *Choctaw Tribune*, to old Choctaw ways at the farm of a condemned murderer. It also brings them to head on clashes with leading townsmen who want their reports silenced no matter what.

More killings are ahead. Who will survive to know the truth? Will truth survive?

The Executions is available on multiple retailer sites.

TRAITORS (CHOCTAW TRIBUNE SERIES, BOOK 2)

"Someone's going to be king in this territory.
No reason it can't be me. It sure won't be you."

Betrayed.

Someone is tearing at the fabric of the Choctaw Nation while political turmoil, assassinations, and feuds threaten the very sovereignty of the tribe. It stands under the U.S. government's scrutiny.

When heated words turn to hot lead, Ruth Ann Teller—a mixed-blood Choctaw—fears losing her brother who won't settle for anything but the truth. Matthew is determined to use his newspaper, the *Choctaw Tribune*, to uncover the scheme behind Mayor Thaddeus Warren's claim to the townsite of Dickens. Matthew is willing to risk his newspaper—and his life—to uncover a traitor among their Choctaw people.

But when Ruth Ann tries to help, she causes more harm than good—especially after the mayor brings in Lance Fuller, a schoolteacher from New York. How does this charming yet aloof young man fit into the mayor's scheme?

When attacks against the newspaper strike and bullets fly, a trip to the Chicago World's Fair of 1893 is the answer they need to save the Choctaw Tribune. The trip holds a key to Matthew's investigation.

But Ruth Ann must find the courage to face a journey to the White City —without her brother.

***Traitors* is available on multiple retailer sites.**

♦♦♦

SHAFT OF TRUTH (CHOCTAW TRIBUNE SERIES, BOOK 3)

"Nothing to it but a stout heart."

On a mission to bring justice to the outlaw gang that murdered his father and brother, Matthew Teller leaves the *Choctaw Tribune* newspaper for his sister to operate and plunges into an unfamiliar world of darkness and danger. Working inside the coal mines of the Choctaw Nation—one of the most dangerous places in the country—he searches for a man who may have the answers to this six-year-old mystery. But after Matthew uncovers an earth-shattering truth that rocks him to his core, he must decide what right is, and what price he is willing to pay for it.

Ruth Ann Teller knows she can handle publishing the *Choctaw Tribune*—until she loses their biggest advertiser. Now, with Matthew miles away and the future of the newspaper resting squarely on her shoulders, Ruth Ann must make a bold move to keep the newspaper afloat in her brother's absence. She sets it on a course for new success or total disaster.

Striking coal miners. Outlaw gangs. An unsolved crime. And a Choctaw family that fights for one another, and for truth.

***Shaft of Truth* (*Choctaw Tribune* Series, Book 3) is available on multiple retailer sites.**

◆◆◆

ANUMPA WARRIOR: CHOCTAW CODE TALKERS OF WORLD WAR I

The day I betrayed Isaac, I vowed never again to speak my native language in front of white men.

When America enters the Great War in 1917, Bertram Robert Dunn and his Choctaw buddies from Armstrong Academy join the army to protect their homes, their families, and their country. Hoping to find redemption for a horrible lie that betrayed his best friend, B.B. heads into the trenches of France—but what he discovers is a duty only his native tongue can fulfill.

War correspondent Matthew Teller is ready to quit until an encounter with a fellow Choctaw sets him on a path to write the untold story of American Indian doughboys. But entrenched stereotypes and prejudices tear at his burning desire to spread truth.

With the Allies building toward the greatest offensive drive of the war, the American Expeditionary Forces face a superior enemy who intercepts their messages and knows their every move. Can the solution come from a people their own government stripped of culture and language?

Anumpa Warrior **is available on multiple retailer sites.**

◆◆◆

TOUCH MY TEARS: TALES FROM THE TRAIL OF TEARS

For this collection of short stories, Choctaw authors from five U.S. states came together to present a part of their ancestors' journey, a way to honor those who walked the trail for their future. These stories not only capture a history and a culture, but the spirit, faith, and resilience of the Choctaw people.

Tears of sadness. Tears of joy. Touch and experience them.

Touch My Tears **is available on multiple retailer sites.**

◆ ◆ ◆

TUSHPA'S STORY (Touch My Tears Collection)

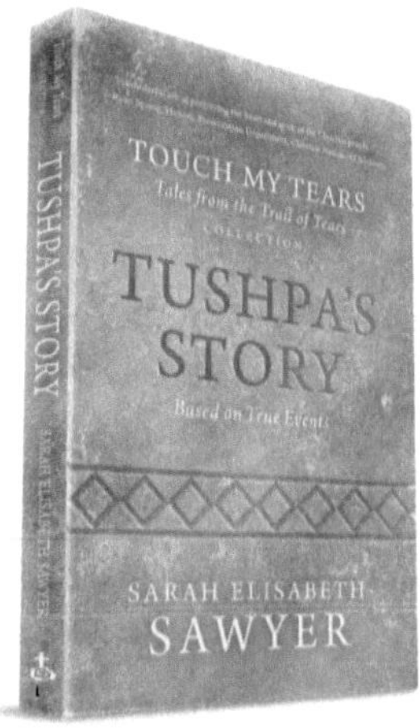

"Protect the book as you do our seed corn. We must have both to survive."

The Treaty of Dancing Rabbit Creek changed everything. The Choctaw Nation could no longer remain in their ancient homelands.

Young Tushpa, his family, and their small band embark on a trail of life and death. More death than life lay ahead.

On their journey to a new homeland, the faith of his father and one book guide Tushpa as he learns what it means to become a man and a leader.

But before long, betrayal from within and without rip at the unity of the band. Can Tushpa help keep his tattered people together? Or will they all be lost to sickness of the mind, body, and spirit on the four hundred mile walk?

A continuation of the anthology *Touch My Tears: Tales from the Trail of Tears*, this story follows an original manuscript written by Tushpa's son, James Culberson.

Tushpa's Story is available on multiple retailer sites.

ABOUT THE AUTHOR

SARAH ELISABETH SAWYER is a story archaeologist. She digs up shards of past lives, hopes, and truths, and pieces them together for readers today. The Smithsonian's National Museum of the American Indian honored her as a literary artist through their Artist Leadership Program for her work in preserving Choctaw Trail of Tears stories. A tribal member of the Choctaw Nation of Oklahoma, she writes historical fiction from her hometown in Texas, partnering with her mother, Lynda Kay Sawyer, in continued research for future works. Learn more at SarahElisabethWrites.com, Facebook.com/SarahElisabethSawyer